PEREZ
l

BARBARA SATTLER
AND
KENNEY
HEGLAND

outskirts
press

Perez and O'Grady, Lawyers

v3.0

This is a work of fiction. Names, characters, businesses, places, events, locales, and incidents are either the products of the author's imagination or used in a fictitious manner. Any resemblance to actual persons, living or dead, or actual events is purely coincidental.

The opinions expressed in this manuscript are solely the opinions of the author and do not represent the opinions or thoughts of the publisher. The author has represented and warranted full ownership and/or legal right to publish all the materials in this book.

Outskirts Press, Inc.
http://www.outskirtspress.com

Paperback ISBN: 978-1-9772-3158-1

PRINTED IN THE UNITED STATES OF AMERICA

KENNEY HEGLAND
1940–2020

All proceeds go to the Kenney F. Hegland Scholarship Fund, James E. Rogers College of Law, University of Arizona

ACKNOWLEDGMENTS

As always, thanks to Meg Park's writing group listed below for all their support and critiques: MaryAnn Pressman, Roslyn Schiffman, Terry Tanner, Marie Trump, Ann Hammond, Beverly Pollock, Robert Samuels, John Jefferies, Bob Lofquist, Linda Greeley, Gene Grazzini, Carla Imray, and Beth Smith.

Special thanks to William Boyd for his suggestions, and to Jodi Weisberg and Mary Lawrence for proofreading and encouragement.

OTHER WORKS BY THE AUTHORS

Barbara Sattler

Dog Days (2013)

Anne Levy's Last Case (2014)

My Name is Molly (2017)

Behind the Robe (2019)

Kenney Hegland

Fiction

Law School Chronicles (2016)

Nonfiction

Introduction to the Study and Practice of Law in a Nutshell (7th Edition) (2017)

Short and Happy Guide to Elder Law, with Robert Fleming (2013)

Short and Happy Guide to Law Practice, with Paul Bennet (2012)

New Times, New Challenges: Law and Advice for Savvy Seniors and Their Families, with Robert Fleming (2009)

Alive and Kicking: Legal Advice for Boomers, with Robert Fleming (2007)

Trial and Clinical Skills in a Nutshell (2006)

Fifty and Beyond: The Law You and Your Parents Need to Know with Allan D. Bogutz (1999)

The Trouble Book (1974)

To what higher object, to what greater character,
Can any mortal aspire to than to be
possessed of all this knowledge,
Well digested and ready at command,
To assist the feeble and friendless,
To discountenance the haughty and lawless,
To procure the redress of wrongs, the advancement of right,
To assert and maintain liberty and virtue,
To discourage and abolish tyranny and vice?
John Adams,
Revolutionary, President, and Lawyer

Law isn't something we know,
It's something we do, like baseball.
Grant Gilmore
Law Professor

PROLOGUE

"You OK, Luce?"

"Yeah," Lucy says—her first of many lies today. Sweat runs down her face, she's nauseous, dizzy, and her body aches. "I'm just tired." Tired of my body hurting, tired of wanting drugs, tired of needing drugs, tired of searching for drugs. Fucking drugs. "I'm going home to get some sleep."

"You can stay here," says Ethel.

"No thanks. Gotta go."

Ethel walks her to the door. They hug. Lucy's aware Ethel watches her as she walks to her car. When she's sure her sister has closed the door, she opens her cell. What name did she put him under? Paul. Dill. No, Phil. Rhymes with pill.

He answers on the second ring. "Yeah."

"It's Ethel." She always uses her sister's name when she talks to dealers. "I need some stuff."

"What stuff?"

"The usual."

"I'm not a mother-fuckin' mind reader."

"Morphine, oxy."

"No pills. Meth?"

"I don't do that."

He hangs up.

Lucy fears Ethel watches her from the window. She starts the car. Her hand shakes. She can hardly dial.

"Nik, it's Ethel. Can you get me some oxy?"

"Sixty pills for a hundred dollars."

"I don't have a hundred dollars. I get paid Friday. I'll pay you then."

Come on, Nik, say yes. Please.

"I'm not the welfare office. You got forty dollars?"

"Yeah."

"I can get you some black powder. Good stuff."

"I don't do needles."

"Smoke it."

She hangs up. Starts to cry.

Drug addicts use heroin. Not women like me. I finished college, law school. None of this was my fault. Not the accident. If the jerk hadn't gone through the red light, I never would've started using.

Shit, where is she? She puts her foot on the brake. The street seems familiar. She's scored here before. Rusted appliances in the front yards. Dead plants. Dogs barking. Run-down houses. Trailers. Guys in hoodies huddled at the corner. She doesn't know how she got here.

Maybe she could go to one of those title loan places. Her car has to be worth something even ten years old, full of dents, broken air. It runs. There's one where the *Dunkin Donuts* used to be. She needs to get out of here.

She rummages through the glove compartment: old insurance cards, repair receipts, gum wrappers, and half of an old oxy pill. She dry swallows, waits for it to take effect. Where's the damn title?

One wonderful hit never hurt anyone.

A knock on the window—A tall bearded man wearing a hoodie. Should she roll down the window? What if he grabs her? She's in a car for god's sake. She can drive away. Where are the damn keys? Did she drop them, put them in the glove compartment?

He knocks again, mimics rolling down the window. She does.

"What do you want?"

"What do *you* want is the question?"

At first she doesn't know what he means. As the pill takes effect her aches and pains recede. Her mind clears.

"I don't have much money."

"What would you want if you did?"

"I don't know you. You could be a cop?"

He bursts into laughter. "Sister, are you fucking kidding me? Cops can't ask. That's entrapment."

Cops lie, but shit, I need it.

"OK, sixty pills oxy, morphine."

"I don't want to talk exposed like this. Take a walk with me."

"I don't think so."

He could rape me, kill me.

"Let me in the car. It's cold out here."

"OK, but I've got a knife."

He laughs again, opens the passenger door, and sits down. "I'm Luke. What's your name?"

"Lucy." Shit. "I mean Ethel."

He looks at her. First her face and then her body up and down. Stares at her necklace—a gold chain with two small rubies for her July birthday.

She feels exposed. Crosses her arms over her chest.

I shouldn't have let him in.

"Trade? I'll give you ten pills."

She isn't that desperate.

"No, I'm not going to do it with you."

"Listen, Lucy honey, I mean Ethel. I don't want a relationship. How about twenty pills? You could blow me or we could have a quickie in the back."

That's all I'm worth? Twenty pills?

"No, get out."

"Relax, you don't want me, fine. I'm not going to force you. I'm not that kind of guy."

"I get paid Friday. I promise I can pay you then."

"How about you give me that necklace?"

"My mom gave it to me for my sixteenth birthday." She'd given the same necklace to her sister when she turned sixteen. Both have July birthdays.

"You expect me to just give you sixty. I don't know you. Give me the necklace for collateral? Meet me here Friday night, at seven, with the money. I'll give it back."

"How do I know you won't sell it?"

"You're worth more as a repeat customer. Wait here." He gets out of the car and walks across the street to a black Escalade. Gets in. Closes the door. He's taking a long time.

I can leave. Go home. Look for the title. Title loan places stay open twenty-four hours a day. I'd be inside with other people. I'd still have my necklace.

A few minutes later Luke walks back to the car holding a bottle of pills. "One hundred dollars plus twenty for the loan."

Why the extra twenty? I better not complain. He might change his mind.

"What is it?"

"Morphine."

"Open the bottle. I want to see it."

He opens the bottle. Hands her one.

"One hundred and twenty milligrams?"

"Yeah."

She looks at the pill, the bottle in his hand. She can't wait to count them, take one or two or three. No, she needs to be careful and make them last.

"Well?" He gestures toward her neck. "I don't have all day."

She takes off the necklace and hands it to him.

"See you Friday, darlin.'" He walks back to his car and drives off.

Her neck feels cold and naked. How stupid? She'd never taken off the necklace since her mom gave it to her. She'd given it to a stranger. Almost given him her body. She's no better than a whore. What if he had crabs or herpes? Syphillis. What if he doesn't show? Her necklace had to be worth more than the pills. Thank goodness her parents are dead. What's she going to tell Ethel if she doesn't get her necklace back?

I need to stop, get clean.

She looks at the pills. She hears them calling, "Take me, take me."

I'll use this bottle and then stop. I'm under too much pressure now. It'll give me time to find a good program. Everything's going to be fine.

She takes one.

One wonderful hit never hurt anyone.

CHAPTER ONE

"Can I speak to Lucy Wagner?"

"It's me."

"This is Angela from Serenity House. We have a place for you tomorrow. Be here at eight a.m. with everything you'll need for the next month or so. Make sure to bring any prescription meds you take. Any questions?"

"No," she says although she has several. Can I leave if I want to? What if I test positive? What's the food like? Do I have to share a room, a bathroom? Can Ethel visit me?

"We have a waiting list as you know. If you aren't here on time we'll give your room to someone else and you'll go to the end of the line."

"I'll be there. I promise."

Deciding to go to Serenity House was the hardest decision she ever made. Maybe second hardest. Telling her sister she'd been abusing opioids and taking heroin was even worse.

Lucy and Ethel were close when they were growing up. Lucy was delighted to have a little sister that she could teach to do things and later play with. They had started drifting apart in their early teens. Every time Lucy answered the phone it was a boy, 'Hi, Lucy, can I talk to Ethel?' Ethel became boy crazy, and although older, Lucy had not yet developed an interest in boys. Or maybe she thought boys weren't interested in her. They drifted further apart when Ethel got married and Lucy went to law school.

The day came when Lucy was desperate. After a thorough search of her car, her apartment, and the laundry room, she'd found less than two dollars. Everything of value had already been pawned. She had no place to live after being evicted for nonpayment of rent. She was hungry and had a persistent cough and skin rashes. She considered stealing food, but a supermarket employee kicked her out before she could try. She looked like a loser. She had no choice but to ask Ethel for help. To tell her she was an addict. The worst didn't happen—in fact, the opposite. Ethel hugged her and promised to help. Ethel insisted Lucy move in with her and her husband, Bob.

Two days later, "Lucy, I've found a residential rehab place in Tucson. It has a wonderful success rate. Bob and I will pay for it. We know you'll pay us back when you can."

Lucy didn't know what to say. Ethel smiled, "With interest."

Ethel's terrific. If it wasn't for her I'd be on the street or dead. Maybe she'd forgive me about the necklace. I was so stupid to be jealous of her. It's all my fault. No matter how tough rehab is I'll make it, for both of us.

At 7:50 a.m. Ethel drops Lucy off in front of Serenity House. She parks her car across the street to make sure Lucy doesn't chicken out. Lucy pauses at the door. She's scared. She doesn't know what to expect. She can't do this. She wants to change her mind, but sees Ethel's car and walks in.

A tall solidly built woman with spikes in her purple hair walks over. "Hi, I'm Bobby-Jo, a counselor here. Let's get you some tea or coffee and a snack. Then you can fill out the intake forms."

By the end of the day, Lucy thinks if any place will help her stop using, it's here. She had tried AA and NA a few times but religion, prayer, and "My name is Lucy, I'm an addict," wasn't her thing. Jesus wasn't going to help her stop.

As a child Lucy had prayed when she wanted a pair of new skates and had gone to church on Sundays with her parents. When she started high school she rebelled. Her parents took the easy path and didn't force her to attend church. Maybe they wanted to sleep in. Lucy never prayed again until the accident. The pain was intense, unrelenting. Her body ached all over, all day, worse at night. She could never get comfortable so she rarely slept. She thought about death.

Dying has to be better.

At the hospital a minister visited and asked her to pray with him. She was too tired to argue. She prayed. God didn't answer. The pain stayed the same. God didn't help her feel better and God wasn't going to help her give up her addiction.

The first days at Serenity House are a blur. The nurse gives her meds to help her detox, but she feels like shit. Jittery, nauseous, out of her body. She can hardly eat. If she had enough energy, she'd leave and get high.

Fuck this place. I can call Phil, get some morphine. I'll need money. The people who work here must have some. I'll find their purses, grab what I can and take off. But Ethel?

"I need to call my sister."

"Sorry," the nurse responds, "we don't allow outside contact the first two weeks. You need to focus on what's going on in here, not out there. Everyone panics at first. Hang in there. Bobby-Jo thinks you'll do great."

Bobby-Jo thinks she'll do great? Lucy feels better. Starts talking in group counseling. She tells about her accident and how it led to opioid abuse.

"I smoked heroin, never shot it. But I was never an addict."

"What a bunch of bullshit." Bobby-Jo's southern twang makes it sound less severe, more understanding.

One of the requirements is to keep a daily journal. It's supposed to help you learn about yourself.

6/19 I hate this place. Everyone always telling you what to do. I want to leave. I'm not a junkie. I'm almost a lawyer. I don't belong here.

6/20 *Why did I give my necklace away? One of the few things I had from mom. I can't tell Ethel the truth. I'll have to make up something.*

6/21 People think you take drugs to get high. I never got high on pain pills. All the pills did was stop the pain when I took enough. If I stopped the pills, I went into withdrawal. That was the worst. Anxiety, nausea, worse pain. I took more drugs to stop withdrawal. I never got high.

She can hear Bobby-Jo's voice, "Stop bullshitting."

6/22 We had a class today about the genetic connection to drug use. Some people take a drink or a pill and they're hooked. Other people can use sometimes. No one in my family drinks too much. I never heard of anyone using drugs. A girl in my group said if addiction is genetic it will make people more understanding, but maybe it's an excuse to keep using.

6/23 Because of drugs I'm not a lawyer even though I passed the bar first try. I still have to pass Character and Fitness. I told the truth about my drug use on the application because I knew if I lied and they found out I'd never be a lawyer.

The food is good and ample. Her only gripe is the dessert is always fruit although it's good for her weight. She likes most of her fellow druggies, although sometimes there seems to be a competition as to who had the worst life.

It figures the one woman she can't stand is her roommate, Sarah, who she nicknames Pollyanna. Pollyanna's taken to rehab in a big way. She goes to the two daily AA meetings held at Serenity House in addition to all the required counseling and classes. Talks a lot in counseling and offers scads of worthless advice. Lucy thinks she's lying about her past. Always volunteers to help set the tables, even do dishes.

7/1 Pollyanna, that Goody Two-Shoes, drives me crazy. She acts like she's trying to be Student of the Week or Camper of the Month. "When you feel like a hit just think of a mountain stream" doesn't help.

Lucy can't wait to get a new roommate. All that rah, rah, rah is too much. She gets her wish. Sarah is kicked out when they find cocaine hidden in a fake soup can in her drawer. No wonder she was cheerful.

"Congratulations, Lucy, you've been clean for fourteen days. You've earned phone privileges."

As soon as the counseling session is over, she calls Ethel.

"Hey, I'm two weeks clean."

"Congratulations, that's terrific. I'm proud of you."

She's proud of me. I can do this.

CHAPTER TWO

Perez and O'Grady is a two-person Tucson law firm. No, make that two-person, one-dog firm. Their website announces it's located in the historic barrio of Tucson, and claims it specializes in every legal area they could think of, including "dog bites." As is the case in historic, picturesque neighborhoods, most of the original owners have been bought out, replaced by professionals. The houses are mostly adobe, many with mesquite fences. A few owners have inherited homes from their parents or grandparents and still live there. Plant gardens or raise chickens. Tell themselves they care about the barrio's history and won't sell out. Until they do. Gentrification is hard to fight.

It's a pretty house, perfect for a law office, the front room converted into the reception area: receptionist, copy machine, chairs for clients. One of the bedrooms became the library and the other two are offices for Frank and Sean. There is a walled-in back porch good for another lawyer, just in case. Its real selling points, however, are it's only two blocks from Superior Court and has a yard for Dusty, the firm dog. The downside: parking is a bitch.

Frank Perez and Sean O'Grady are in their early thirties and Dusty is around four in people years, according to the Humane Society.

It's not often that a skinny fourteen-year-old, who looked twelve, can take credit for the birth of a law firm. But it happens. Arturo Contreras was one of several minors arrested for manslaughter after what the police called a "gang fight" resulted in a teen dying when he fell and hit his head.

When a person under eighteen is arrested for a serious crime the issue is whether to try him as a juvenile or an adult. If convicted as a juvenile he can be incarcerated only until he is eighteen, but if convicted as an adult he faces decades in prison. Sean, Arturo's lawyer, was trying to keep him in juvenile court and not sent downtown.

"Arturo is a decent kid, never been in trouble. Doing well in school. Lives with his parents who are concerned and supportive. Hopes to be a Navy pilot. Wasn't taking part in the fight, which was, by the way, a typical high school fight, not a gang fight. Whatever the outcome in juvenile court it's better for him than sitting in prison for years listening to hardened criminals."

Sean's arguments fell on deaf ears. Henderson, a prosecutor in juvie, responded, "We are going to try him as an adult. He's a bad actor—tattoos. We have to send a message."

Shit, I'll call Frank, my old friend from law school. He knows the difference between a bad ass and a kid in the wrong place at the wrong time. This "sending messages" is bullshit. No one is paying attention to what happens in court. Criminals don't read the newspaper and don't worry about what will happen if they get caught, because they think they won't get caught.

After law school Frank had taken a job as a prosecutor and rose quickly to be in charge of juvenile transfers to adult court. He had more sense than Henderson.

"I'll have him back off. Tell him we could never convict the kid rather than tell him he's an idiot. Have your guy plead to something like 'disturbing an educational facility.' We'll recommend community service."

Done.

Frank and Sean decided to get a beer to catch up on law school classmates and bitch about the law. Soon it became clear both were unhappy with their jobs and Arturo's unintended consequence came to be.

Perez and O'Grady became their own bosses, taking only the cases they want, defending the downtrodden, fighting injustice, getting rich.

Ha.

First the expenses: rent, website, computers, desks, chairs, refrigerator, malpractice insurance, coffee pot or two in the unlikely event someone drinks decaf.

The best thing they did was hire Cindy. She had worked a few years for a solo practitioner who had recently retired. Frank knew criminal law and Sean juvenile law, but neither knew much about the nuts and bolts of practice—how long you have to answer a contract complaint, what to expect when you file a claim with an insurance company, how to schedule a deposition, or how vague you can be answering interrogatories. Cindy had been there, done that, and was invaluable.

After a few years of struggle, living off referrals from other lawyers and court appointments, things were hopping and they decided to get another lawyer. Their website was a huge disappointment, except for two dog bite cases, and the third, a crank call, someone claiming to be a pit bull falsely accused.

CHAPTER THREE

Lucy parks her eight-year-old Honda a few blocks from the law office of Perez and O'Grady. She doubts her banged up car will make the right impression. And making the right impression is crucial. She wants this job—no, *needs* this job.

She works at the public defender's office. She loves the people and the excitement, but because she isn't a member of the bar, she only writes memos for those who are. She's good at it. However, delving into questions like "Do police need probable cause to search your dumpster?" is not her cup of tea and she's pretty sure criminal law is not for her. Not to mention there are no benefits and the salary is barely more than minimum wage.

Since her successful rehab she's lived in her own apartment and has made her sister proud. But, due to high rent and low income, she hasn't seen a doctor in over two years, and can't remember her last dentist visit.

Don't appear too anxious. But don't act like you think you're doing them a favor.

Her day got off to a rotten start. She'd gained weight and couldn't zip up her favorite dress or even her second favorite. In spite of the hot weather she'd put on her navy-blue wool suit. The long jacket enabled her to use safety pins to close the waistband. Hardly noticeable, she hopes. Her brown hair looked fine when she left the house, but when she checks the mirror it's frizzing up. She walks slowly, carrying her briefcase, hoping to look professional, balancing the need to be on time against appearing or, worse, smelling sweaty.

She's on time. Cindy, the firm's secretary/receptionist/

fashion consultant, greets her.

"The lawyers are running late. Can I make you some coffee or get you some water, Ms. Wagner?"

"Call me Lucy. I'm good."

"The lawyers must have been impressed with you, Lucy. Lots of people applied."

Is she kidding? Why would they take a chance on a recovering addict? How did this small firm snag Cindy?

She's a knockout dressed in a form-fitting red dress, matching scarf, and stiletto red heels that compliment her complexion. She has long dark hair, large brown eyes, and a figure most women would covet. And she seems nice.

Lucy wonders how a secretary can afford such fashionable clothing. At the public defender's office she wears whatever she likes. She has no client contact, rarely any personal contact, and works in a cubicle. Jeans and a collared shirt are good enough. Ross is her go-to store. Nordstrom Rack for special occasions. She can't remember the last time she had a special occasion. Even the women lawyers at the PD's office don't dress as well as Cindy.

I shouldn't be wasting time thinking about Cindy. A partner might walk in. Professionals never only sit, waste time. Look busy.

Lucy opens her briefcase and starts proofreading a memorandum, at least pretends to. A partner might walk in.

A buzz. Cindy picks up. "Lucy, they're ready for you. Good luck." Cindy gives her a thumbs up.

"Lucy, thanks for coming." Frank sits at a small table in his office. "Have a seat. Has Cindy offered you a drink? Water, soda, or coffee—we even have decaf."

"No, I'm fine."

"After our phone call I thought it would be good for you to come in and meet my partner Sean and talk about a job."

Sean, tall, slender, good-looking, smiles. "We're impressed with your resume; good grades, almost as good as Frank's."

Frank shakes his head. It's clear they like each other.

"I heard from Professor Finer you did a bang-up job in the Criminal Law Clinic. We do some of that but we're a general practice firm. We're looking for an associate and you might fit the bill."

Might as well get it over with.

"I told you my bar status on the phone."

"Yeah, we know a lot of people who abused drugs and no longer do," Frank says and then adds, "I'm Catholic and believe in forgiveness."

"I'm not," says Sean, "but I do too. As long as they can stay off drugs."

Stay positive. Don't get defensive. You've done a lot.

"I've been clean almost two years and intend to stay that way. I plan on reapplying and I think I've got a good chance."

"We'd be counting on you staying clean. Your boss at the public defender tells me you are a good writer and researcher and if they had a position it would be yours. Mary Doyle had high praise for the senior paper you wrote, 'The Legal Aspects of *The Merchant of Venice.*' One of the best defenses of Shylock she's read."

"It was in 'Law and Literature.' Professor Doyle was terrific."

"No shit, excuse my French—Law and Literature?' They never had that when I was a student. Maybe I would've ended up as an English teacher. I've always thought Shylock got a raw deal."

"We have to ignore Sean's existential moments," laughs Frank. "Early midlife crisis."

"I've heard great things about your firm," Lucy blurts out.

Again, don't be too anxious.

"We'd like to offer you a job and see how things work out. We can't guarantee anything permanent."

"Understood."

"When we have a big project we work nights and weekends. But we're pretty loose on personal time and sick time."

"Not a problem."

I'm seldom sick.

"We'll pay fifty thousand dollars, plus healthcare. I assume you'd want to give at least two weeks notice at the PD? Do you need time to think about it?"

Screw the advice. I'm anxious. Fifty thousand and benefits?

"No, I'm in. I'll give my notice today."

CHAPTER FOUR

Lucy gives her two-week notice as soon as she gets back to the office. She's surprised when she realizes how much she'll miss her colleagues—and more surprised they'll miss her. A good-bye party is scheduled at the Shanty Bar, a PD hangout, after work on her last day.

The Shanty's located on the outskirts of downtown, popular with prosecutors, defenders, legal aid types, and even some in suits with briefcases—partnership material but still wanting to have fun rather than another raise. Couple of pool tables, an outside patio, no flat screens, and no need to smile and nod—you can actually hear what's being said. The last bar fight is legend (or myth) and women need not worry (too much) about their safety. Lucy sits on the patio, cool even in summer. Lots of trees and shade. Most of the tables are filled, laughter and good times. Colleagues offer beers and wish her good luck.

Be careful. Alcohol triggers drug use.

She sips.

Brian, who hasn't been sipping, stumbles over.

"Sure quitting is a good idea?"

What does he want except for what drunks usually want?

Lucy says nothing. Brian is stuck. He'd thought some small talk would lead up to "Let's go do it." Now that seems a little abrupt. "O'Grady and Perez aren't the most ethical. O'Grady's always close to the line, maybe over."

This from Mr. Sleaze? O'Grady's the good looking one.

"It's Perez and O'Grady. It's a done deal."

Mr. Sleaze never had a Plan B; he stumbles away.

"Something the matter?" Lisa, one of the office stars and Lucy's hero, walks over. "You don't look happy."

"Brian told me Perez and O'Grady have issues."

"Mr. Sleaze? He's been out to get Sean for years and no doubt wanted to keep you from joining his firm. Sean destroyed him in moot court. Come get some cake. Brian's an asshole."

A large white cake with chocolate frosting, the "*Congrats*" already eaten. Lisa, who couldn't be more than a size two, that and a terrific trial lawyer (damn her), cuts two big pieces of cake and hands one to Lucy.

Lucy doesn't want cake. Trying to diet. She'll save money if she can fit into her old clothes.

Screw it, one piece of cake never hurt anyone. I won't eat breakfast.

Clay walks in. Lucy hasn't had a crush since high school but that changed when she met Clay, one of the office appellate lawyers. He has curly brown hair, large green eyes and a shyness about him she finds adorable. She had asked him for help a few times on motions she was writing. He was helpful but always kept the conversation professional.

"Why don't you just ask him out?" Lucy's sister Ethel said at their last lunch. "Times they're a changing."

"I gained so much weight. I doubt anyone would be interested in me. Who wants a fat drug addict?"

"You're crazy. You've been clean a long time. You've got to get over this drug addict stuff. It's not you. Once someone gets to know you they'll love you. You've got a great sense of humor. And you're not fat."

Lucy laughed. "That's what they said about fat girls in high school, 'she's a lot of fun to be with.' "

But maybe Ethel's right.

I won't be seeing him at work. He's cutting a piece of cake. It's now or never.

Lucy walks toward him. Thankfully he's the first to talk. "Hey Lucy, I'm sorry you're leaving. I enjoyed working with you."

"Thanks. It's not like I'm leaving town. The firm is only a couple blocks away."

Shit, I sound desperate.

"So what do you have planned for this weekend?"

This weekend? Is he serious? Nothing. Laundry, give Teddy a bath, watch Netflix, go without breakfast.

"I'm pretty tied up."

"I was thinking maybe we could get together tomorrow night, see a movie."

Everyone is busy on Saturday night. If I say, no he might never ask again.

"This Saturday night? I was going to my sister's for dinner but she just canceled. A movie would be fun. I'd like that."

"Great. I'll give you a call after I check the movie times."

Both fall silent, too little or too much to say.

Clay smiles and walks back to the bar. Lucy floats to the patio. She chats with colleagues and catches up on gossip and jokes.

"No, I didn't know they had a fight and, no, I hadn't heard that one, funny."

She leaves as soon as she can, before Clay can change his mind or Brian can try again.

Great party, wonderful friends, a date with Clay, only half a beer, and to hell with the cake, it wasn't that good.

CHAPTER FIVE

The phone rings.

"Shit. Answer it, Frank."

The red numerals on the clock announce 3:17 a.m.

"Frank, this is Paul Nash, sorry to wake you, but my son's been arrested."

Frank turns to his wife, puts his hand over the cell, and whispers, "It's Paul, my old golf partner." Marie remembers him as an arrogant jerk who treated his wife like a child. She was always a better judge of character than Frank. He'd never admit that.

"Oh yeah, Paul. Your son, Jordan? Arrested for what?"

"Some bitch he met at his frat party claims he raped her. She led him on and he didn't do anything and his mom's frantic and— ... "

"Relax, Paul. Is Jordan in jail?"

"Yeah, he's only twenty. He'll be killed or raped. He's never been in jail. No one in our family has. Can you go see him? Not as a favor. I'll pay."

"I can try to get him out, try to calm him down. I'll be there in an hour. We can talk fees in the morning."

Marie smiles. She knows arrogant jerk is loaded. She turns over and goes back to sleep.

Frank puts on his jeans, pulls on a clean short-sleeved collared shirt, and heads out on a cool, still dark morning. He used to wear a suit when he made a jail visit, but he realizes few defense lawyers dress up at night so he opts for comfort.

Jordan must be terrified. Worst night of his life. Behind bars with drunks, gangbangers, psychopaths, loud shouts, and curses. Guards with guns. Not knowing what will happen, next week, next few minutes. A big part of my job is being with clients in scary times like doctors used to.

It's a good half hour to the jail. The streets, except for the red lights, are deserted. Frank likes being a lawyer. He remembers his first days in law school.

It was a large stadium-type classroom, ten elevated rows, three sections, permanent chairs, long work tables, assigned seats, 110 alert and eager students each one, Frank knows, smarter, more articulate, more knowledgeable than he is.

I'm the dumbest one here. I'll flunk out. Please don't call on me.

The man in the pit, bowtie sports coat, elbow patches, a god who knows everything strutted back and forth, occasionally stopping at the podium to pick out, after a pregnant pause, his next victim.

Silence. No nervous chattering. No shuffling of papers. Silence. Then:

"Ms. Meek, the case of *Brown v. Finney*."

Ms. Meek seemed to have gotten the drift.

Unbelievable. She knows not only that Brown won, but why he won. I never understood why. I spent an hour reading and rereading that case and all I got out of it was Brown and Finney in 1878 met at a bar in Ohio, made a deal about Finney selling coal to Brown but Finney never delivered.

After her amazing performance, which confirmed Frank's worse fears, Ms. Meek asked Bowtie whether Brown got his coal.

Good question.

Apparently not.

"Ms. Meek, we don't care!" puffed Bowtie showing that even if you get something right, he'll show you how you're wrong. "We're only interested in why he should have gotten the coal."

OK, we don't care about the people or what happens to them. They're only bit players illustrating a legal rule. Fine with me.

"What if the deal wasn't made in a bar?"

But it was made in a bar!

Ms. Meek, no longer so smart, froze, and Bowtie stopped,

paused, "Mr . . ." Frank held his breath, looked down.

Never make eye contact.

"Mr . . . Ryan."

Thank God, the hour's almost up.

Mr. Ryan was on top of things, argued it wouldn't matter if the deal wasn't in a bar, making points Frank never would have thought of.

Good to know, it doesn't matter.

But wait! Ms. King raised her hand, and made a compelling argument why it would matter.

Who is right?

Bowtie simply smiled and asked another question. "What if the contract is for a perishable product?"

Shit!

The Socratic Method: never answers, only questions.

"What if the landlord had installed a light, but someone shot it out?"

"What if the defendant was drunk when he confessed?"

"What if they agreed to write it down but forgot?"

"What if the dog was an alligator?"

It was chaos. Exhausting. Ideas flying. Everyone was so smart. The guy next to him went to Harvard. Maybe they all went to Harvard.

I'd never thought of that. I have nothing to say. Everything I think is obvious, has been thought of by everyone. Don't call on me.

At the "Welcome to Law School" picnic, "You are only here because you're Mexican," smirked a classmate wearing a Stanford T-shirt—a *well-worn* Stanford T-shirt.

Do all of my classmates think that? Maybe they're right. I should have taken that job in the bank.

Pulling into the jail parking lot Frank remembers how things worked out. He graduated near the top of his class. Well-worn Stanford T-shirt flunked out. He had become comfortable in class and even raised his hand, realizing the things he thought of were as unique as those thought of by the Harvard guys. He learned the critical importance of good questions. Dogs never become alligators, but asking if they did tells you a lot about dogs.

Best of all he met Marie second year.

"Must be a lucrative case to get you up this time of the night," says the guard, name tag "Jill Davis." Frank, now an old-timer, knows most of the jail staff, none as good-looking as Jill.

"Hopefully lucrative. It won't be a long wait?"

"You're the only attorney here, and your guy's still in the holding pen, with any luck less than ten." Most of the newly arrested will be released in the morning. No reason to give them a cell, bedding, and a jumpsuit if they aren't going to be long-term guests.

Why is such a good-looking woman working the night shift at the jail? Not for the poor pay.

Frank hands his briefcase to Jill and goes through the metal detector. The first few times he went to the jail he worried. Alone with a prisoner, maybe violent, maybe mentally ill. It's not comforting to see guards, with guns, standing behind protective glass.

Do they give a shit about attorneys or would they rather have an interesting story to entertain their family with when they get home?

Now it's routine. No beeps. Jill hands him his briefcase. An unseen guard buzzes him through two sets of doors; the second opens after the first closes. He walks down an eerily quiet long hall with numerous security cameras. He reaches the corridor with seven attorney booths. He chooses the middle one.

I wonder how he'll like having a Mexican lawyer.

CHAPTER SIX

The door opens and a tall, handsome young man in obvious distress enters wearing designer jeans and a T-shirt with a frat logo.

"Jordan? I don't know if you remember me, I'm Frank Perez. I play golf with your dad."

"Sure, I remember you. My dad says you're a great lawyer. Thanks for coming."

This guy's too young to pick up a felony conviction. It'll ruin his life. I could've got one when I was about his age and it would've ruined mine.

"Your dad has hired me to represent you if that works for you. Let me tell you a few things to start. You'll have to stay the night here but most likely get out tomorrow. If the prosecutor goes ahead with this, there won't be a trial for months. Don't worry, you won't go back to jail, if at all, until after your trial. The cops can't question you unless I'm there. I know this is confusing. I will answer any questions and I'll be with you during all of this."

"Thanks," Jordan says, "but I just want to get out of here."

Frank smells alcohol.

"I'm sure you do, but I need to explain a few things. You'll see a judge tomorrow. You'll be in a courtroom here at the jail. The judge will be downtown, but you'll see him and he'll see you. Video hookup. It's a short hearing, but important. Bail will be set or you will be released on your own recognizance."

Jordan, who hasn't been paying much attention, asks, "So I'll get out?"

"I'll know better after I get some information. First of all, everything you tell me is confidential. I can't tell anyone what you tell me, not the cops, the prosecutor, or your family. Even though your dad is paying, I'm not his lawyer. I'm yours. I won't tell him anything you don't want him to know. You'll be making the decisions not your dad."

"Good luck with that," Jordan smiles for the first time.

Frank lets that pass. His dad thinks he knows everything. He often tells people which club to use.

"Don't talk to anyone about your case, especially in here. The phones have recording devices and every inmate is looking for someone to snitch on to get a better deal. If anyone asks just say, 'I'm innocent, but my lawyer doesn't want me to talk.' You understand?"

The seriousness of the matter is sinking in. It's not only about getting out in the morning.

"Yes, sir."

"Have you ever been arrested before?"

"I had a DUI a year ago, right after I turned seventeen. I pled guilty."

"Do you have a drinking problem? You smell of alcohol."

"No, I don't have a problem."

"I've heard that a lot. Alcohol doesn't lead only to DUI, but domestic violence and vehicular homicide. Tell you what. I'll give you a list of treatment centers. They're great at helping people who don't think they have a problem."

"I don't. I'm not an alcoholic," Jordan is offended. "Just a few on the weekend."

Frank waves that off. "Let's say, heaven forbid, you are convicted. When it comes to sentencing it will help to tell the judge you've turned your life around, got into treatment. Rehab might help your case but more importantly it might save your life."

Jordan isn't thinking the way Frank wants. "If I was drunk is that a defense?"

He's smarter than his dad.

"Nope, voluntary intoxication never is. And if she was drunk she can't give legal consent."

"Neither of us were drunk. You've got to help me. The people in here stink and stare at me. I'm afraid."

"Tell me what happened. Not all the details, just a summary. But if you tell me you raped her, I won't let you testify that you didn't. I can't put on a witness I know will lie. What happened?"

"There was a party at the frat house. I invited Abby. I've been wanting to ask her out. We drank some beer. Smoked some pot. People were making out all over. It was loud. We wanted to talk. We went into one of the bedrooms. Started making out. One thing led to another. But it wasn't rape. She wanted it as much as I did."

"So you thought she was consenting?"

"Yeah, she was. I don't know what she told the cops, but they arrested me for rape."

"Did they read you your rights?"

"Yeah. Like TV. The cop asked if I was at a party tonight and if I had intercourse with Abby." Jordan falls silent. "I lied, told her I didn't. Stupid, I was scared. But then I came clean. That should count for something."

"Did you admit it only after they told you they'll have DNA evidence to prove you did?"

Jordan looks down, hesitates. "I don't remember."

"They will. Let's move on. Are you in school, working?"

"I'm a junior. I caddy at my dad's golf club."

Rich kid's job. Doubt he ever worked with his hands.

"OK, there's a good chance you'll be released tomorrow. If they set bond it will be low enough that your parents can get you out. Now what did I tell you about talking about your case?"

"My dad will insist."

"I'll call him and lay down the law. Phone my office and set up an appointment in a week or two. I'll read the police reports and talk with the DA's office. They usually aren't eager to prosecute if the girl willingly went to a bedroom and started making out. Juries don't convict. But with the #MeToo movement, who knows? And the DA is running for reelection and won't want to look soft on sexual assault."

"But politics shouldn't matter."

Way smarter.

"Welcome to the real world, Jordan. And those guys locked up with you? They'll probably be asleep when you get back. Their smell is worse than their bite."

On the drive back, hoping for French toast, Frank realizes he might not be popular defending a guy accused of rape. Particularly if he wins. He smiles.

You ain't a real lawyer until you walk into a courtroom and everyone hates you.

CHAPTER SEVEN

After a few weeks at Perez and O'Grady Lucy settles in. She even has her own office, albeit a rather small one, but there is a window. On the credenza are her favorite pictures. Ethel, her mom, and her standing in front of the sea wall at San Diego's Mission Beach. In large letters someone had written "Zoners go home.' Reminds her of many happy summer vacations. Next to it, a wedding picture of her mom and dad. Neither of the girls knew their dad, he died shortly after Ethel was born. And she has two pictures of Teddy, one as a playful pup and the other looking directly at the camera with those pleading, *another treat please*, brown eyes. She hasn't put up her diplomas; the one from law school might trigger embarrassing questions about why she isn't a lawyer.

It's a busy but fun place to work. Clients, some with crying babies, sit in the lobby, phones ring, and deadlines loom. There's even a dog, Dusty. Maybe someday, if things work out, she can bring Teddy. Cindy is fabulous and Lucy has learned if she has a question, even a legal one, to go to her first. Better not to bother your boss. Frank is almost fatherly and is the one running the business side of the practice. Sean, the good-looking one, is fine with that. He's friendly, perhaps too friendly, but Lucy picks up vibes that Sean and Cindy have some kind of relationship. Good or bad she can't tell.

Lucy's introduced as "our law clerk" and asked to sit alertly in one of the partner's office when they want to impress a client. Ironically, she spends most of her day in the firm's library working on legal memos. But the pay is better and there is a chance she'll go to court. There's always coffee, soft drinks in the fridge, pastries to be resisted, and a load of work. Both Frank and Sean had put off doing their own research, waiting until they had someone to do it for them. She's always happy to get out of the office to pick up police reports or research records at the courthouse.

"Hey, Lucy, you busy?" Sean has his briefcase.

"Busy? You said you needed the Henderson memo this afternoon."

"Forget the memo. I'm going to court to get an order of protection. Come along to see what they're like. And then take a long lunch."

I've heard about orders of protection. I'll text Clay. Lunch will likely work. One perk of being an appellate lawyer is you can eat lunch anytime you like since you rarely have a court appearance.

"This is pretty routine," explains Sean. "Her husband probably won't show up and after Ella tells her story the judge will issue an order telling him to stay away from her."

"What good does that do?"

"If he goes to her home or work the police can arrest him for violating the order, he needn't commit a crime. Not that protective orders solve everything. The husband, boyfriend, whoever, may not obey it and sometimes when the person is served with the order he'll get enraged and up the level of violence."

The client is a slight African American woman about forty-five. She's the manager at a Subway and her husband, back from military service, suffers from PTSD, self medicates with bourbon, and is abusive. Sean is handling her divorce. Her husband has moved out but keeps harassing her at work and home.

Ella and Lucy sit outside the courtroom waiting for her case to be called. Sean is off chatting with other lawyers.

"Are you a lawyer?" asks Ella.

"Hope to be."

Why hold back? I too have suffered.

"I'm a recovering drug addict."

"Girl," laughs Ella, "We're all recovering from something. With me it's Martin."

For the next half hour the two exchange war stories and even cry a little. There is so much misery in the world. They'll stay in touch.

The hearing goes as Sean predicted. Ella gets her order. Sean hands it to a sheriff's deputy to serve on Martin. Ella and Lucy hug and she heads off to lunch with Clay.

"Hey girl, good to see you," Clay says as Lucy makes her way to the table.

"Girl?" Lucy smiles. "That's the second time I've been called that today."

"Is 'sexy woman' better?"

"Is that all you think about?"

Their first, second, and third dates went very well. Now they sleep at each other's places. Rarely does a night go by when they don't have sex.They're still excited to talk about favorite movies, books, and restaurants. Their excitement has not collapsed into "how's your day?" But still, it's only been a few dates.

Will this last? Lead to anything? Do I want it to or is it only sex? Is he dating others? Does he want kids?

CHAPTER EIGHT

"Harold Olsen, your one-thirty is here, Mr. O'Grady." Cindy buzzes. *"Mr. O'Grady*?" It's "Hey Sean" except in front of clients.

"Bring him in, in five."

Look busy. Pick up the phone.

Sean knew hiring Cindy had been a great move. He wouldn't admit it, but even before they interviewed her he wanted to hire her. No, he wanted to go out with her and . . . The minute she walked into the office he was dazzled. He knew Frank was looking for something different, a good work ethic and competence. Her looks might be a minus. Cindy turned out to have all the skills they wanted and more, plus good references. Both agreed she was the best candidate. They hired her on the spot.

Five minutes later, Cindy knocks on his door. Sean picks up the phone. As Harold Olsen walks in Sean says, "I told you my client won't plead to anything. Not even a misdemeanor. It's a complete dismissal or we're going to trial."

Sean looks up. "Have a seat, Mr. Olsen."

This guy looks loaded.

He's about six feet two, one-hundred-ninety pounds, his biceps almost busting out of his shirt. Must be a gym rat. He's stylishly dressed, his jeans cost more than a month's car payment.

Sean sits behind his big desk, open computer on one side, a stack of files, mostly for show, on the other. On the wall are the traditional diplomas, including one attesting that he won the eighth grade tennis tournament. He is very proud of that and, at a distance, it looks like yet another academic achievement.

"I'm in deep trouble. Been arrested for a major drug deal."

This may be the big one. Eighty thousand in student debt.

Eighty thousand. Sean has been waiting for a big one: a major car wreck, a bitter divorce, a client dying of lung cancer who smoked Camels. A major drug bust might be the one.

"I've handled numerous drug cases," says Sean. Most were simple possession cases resulting in dismissals with community service or Say No to Drug classes. Never a large sales case. Major dealers make more in a week than he makes in a year, but he's been warned it's somewhat risky representing them. Unsatisfied, they don't file malpractice suits, don't complain to the state bar, but do something more immediate, more direct.

"What do they claim you sold?"

"It's total bullshit. I'm a realtor." He hands Sean a card. Heavy white stock gold lettering, *Olsen Realty, Harold Olsen, President.* "They searched a house I was going to sell when the remodel was done. Found several hundred bottles of pills, oxycontin, morphine, blue Mex, some cash and something they called a ledger. Lots of people had access to the house."

"Did they have a warrant to search the house?"

"Yeah. It said a guy named Jesus gave them some information they used to get the warrant."

"Do you know him?"

"A little. He works with a crew I use to keep the properties up."

"First thing we'll do is check to see if we can get the search warrant quashed. If we can they can't use any evidence they found at the house and the case will go away. To justify a warrant the cops need information from a reliable informant. Maybe we can show this Jesus was unreliable, someone they shouldn't believe."

"Before he gave up the house they threatened to have him deported. Can they do that?"

Can they?

"I'll have my investigator run down Jesus and we'll see."

A knowing smile. Harold's been to this rodeo. "What we got to do is get rid of the rat."

Get rid of? Surely he means at trial, make him out to be a liar.

"Let's see what he has to say. Do you have any release conditions?"

"No, my brother bonded me out."

"How much was your bond."

"Seventy-five thousand dollars." Harold hands him a piece of paper.

Holy shit. His brother posted $75,000 cash. What should I charge this guy? Don't ask if he wants to retain us. Just act like he already has.

Sean picks up the phone, "Cindy, could you bring me a retainer agreement?"

"Mr. Olsen, if the case doesn't go to trial, it'll be twenty-five thousand. That's for pretrial motions, investigation, and general prep. Trial is an additional forty-five thousand, plus expenses. I'll need a ten-thousand-dollar retainer."

Olsen takes his out his wallet and writes a check —for $25,000.

Shit. I should have charged more.

"Is your secretary seeing anyone? I notice she isn't wearing a ring. But these days you can never tell."

"She's seeing someone long term; they're practically engaged."

I hope that's not true.

After Olsen leaves Sean strolls into Frank's office. He is sitting behind his desk, phone to his ear, engaged in a serious conversation. Frank waves him to take a seat. Sean shakes his head, walks around to the back of Frank's desk, and puts the $25,000 check in front of him.

"I'll call you back."

Sean takes a seat.

"This comes at a good time. That was our accountant, the well's going dry. Who's Harold Olsen?"

"Kind of a slimy guy who apparently is a big-time drug lord who needs our help and can pay. If this goes to trial, another $45,000."

"You don't have to like them as long as their checks don't bounce. What's your plan?"

"We need to run down a guy named Jesus who gave Harold up. If the cops threatened him to do it maybe we can quash the warrant."

"I'll put Sam on it, he's gotten great results for me. I worked with cops as a DA and they can get pretty rough getting their information. But I don't remember any cases where a search warrant was thrown out because the cops abused an informant."

"If it was bad enough it's worth a try. This chair sucks."

"Did you come to discuss your case or come to complain?"

"Lucy can research warrant cases. Maybe she'll find something that can lead to a lot more drug cases."

"Not so fast, Sean. An occasional drug case is fine but I don't want this firm being known as a drug firm. I'm not a big fan of their business. I'm more interested in developing our civil practice."

Good. My mom was happy when I was working at Juvenile Hall. Not so happy if she learns I'm lawyer for the mob. But trashing husbands isn't a lot better. And we need the money.

"I agree, but let's get our firm more in the black. Get a new chair." Sean gets up to leave and suddenly it hits him.

"Given Lucy's drug problem do you think she'll be happy working to spring Harold?"

"She's a trooper. She'll do a great job." Frank pauses. "But if Harold's drugs kill one of her friends, watch out."

CHAPTER NINE

Today is the Serenity House's Tenth Annual Fundraiser. Lucy has never gone to the event before and isn't sure what to expect. It's held at an upscale downtown hotel. During law school Lucy went to a fancy wedding there, but she hasn't been to the hotel since. The food was memorable: shrimp cocktail, beef Wellington, baked Alaska. Best meal she ever ate. She hopes her navy suit, which no longer needs a safety pin to button the waist, will make the right impression—lawyer on the way up, not recovering addict.

She stops at a small crowded reception table to pick up her name tag and table assignment. She's at table number eleven. Lucy hopes it's not in the front and that she knows someone seated there.

I don't do well talking to strangers. I'll embarrass myself. I've got to do better. Good lawyers have to talk to all kinds of people they don't know. I've got to stop being such a wuss. I'm smart. I have a law degree.

The banquet room is crowded. Tables are close together. It's hard to walk around without bumping into someone. Multicolored flower arrangements grace each table. They're gorgeous. Lucy notices a few men but mostly women. No jeans or shorts. Some wear expensive dresses, other dressy slacks and shirts, and a few women, like her, wear business suits.

Lucy had been a client in Serenity House's inpatient drug program. It saved her life. Her 9/11 began with an auto accident, the truck speeding toward her forever seared in her memory. Prescription pain meds. Soon she was hooked and abusing opioids.

When she could no longer afford the pills, she tried heroin. She told herself she wasn't an addict. She never shot up, never used needles, only smoked it. Her recovery started when she admitted it didn't matter how she used heroin. She was, is, an addict.

Lucy remembers the moment that led her to Serenity House. She was completely broke, had maxed her credit cards, owed everyone she knew, and had almost traded her body for a fix. Instead, she traded the necklace her mom had given her for her sixteenth birthday. She never saw it again. Time to get help. Now, thanks to her sister and Serenity House, she's almost two years clean.

Graduates of Serenity House are invited to the fundraiser. Even get a free ticket. The ninety-dollar cost would be tough on those struggling with recovery. And everyone struggles. Lucy's luckier than most. She has a job. She had never before considered going. Lucy wants to see friends from rehab, but she's afraid to run into people she knows professionally. Many lawyers attend fundraisers, fundraisers generate clients. She doesn't want them to know she'd been—no, is—an addict, a recovering addict.

Joyce, who she'd met in rehab, is one of the speakers. She'd called Lucy and asked her to be there for moral support. Lucy was unable to say no. They'd been very close, knew each other's struggles, victories, and defeats.

Lucy locates table eleven near the back. A spinach salad is on each plate, and in the middle, a tray of small cakes, maybe petit fours. She wonders what the main course will be. Alas, spinach salad *is* the main course.

Lucy knows half of the women at the table from rehab. She's glad to see them. She doubts they would show up if they were still using. Joyce comes over to say hi and introduces Lucy to two older, well-dressed ladies at the table. She immediately forgets both their names. She assumes they are there to be seen, society ladies. Professional do-gooders. They have no idea what she and the others have gone through, but they'll write checks, which, after all, is the purpose of this event.

"Lucy, you look terrific. What are you doing now?" asks Sandra, a friend from rehab.

"Working at a downtown law firm." Doesn't mention she isn't a lawyer . . . yet. She's saved from further conversation when the first speaker is introduced.

I better watch what I say. Don't want to get caught in a lie.

The director of Serenity House, Ellie Rosenblatt, takes the microphone. She lauds the successes they've had this year and ends with a pitch to donate. Lucy steals a glance at the women Joyce introduced to her.

One has taken a donation envelope from the middle of the table. The other follows.

Lucy listens with half an ear to the rest of the program until Joyce takes the stage.

Wow. I can't believe this healthy, well-dressed, well-groomed person is the skinny, smelly Joyce I knew in rehab.

Serenity House was Joyce's fifth try and, while everyone has a tough time getting through, Joyce was always on the verge of getting kicked out. Lucy isn't sure she believes in God and miracles, but Joyce's sobriety is a miracle.

"My name is Joyce. I grew up in an upper-middle-class home, went to private schools, and had every advantage a child could ask for. Addiction can happen to anyone. It's color blind, gender blind, and class blind. My mom stayed home with me and my brother. My dad was an accountant. My parents drank every night, cocktails before dinner, wine with dinner, and a variety of drinks till bedtime. All their friends did too. I assumed everyone did. My brother is an engineer. Drinks socially. Never had a problem with addiction."

Lucy notices one of the older women at the table crying and later learns her teenage son died of an overdose.

"I drank beginning about age fourteen. Put vodka in my water bottle in high school. In college I smoked pot, then snorted coke. But I still did well in school. It wasn't until my senior year that I met Rick. We did meth once and I was hooked. I loved it. I dropped out of school and moved in with Rick. We preferred meth, but did every drug we could find—opium, LSD, mushrooms, ecstasy. My parents stopped supporting me. Rick had no money and neither of us could hold a job."

Lucy knows how that goes. Different stories, different drugs, then detox, jail, rehab, relapse, but the outcome is the same—stop or die.

"Rick and I stole from our families, friends, and stores. My parents wouldn't let me in the house. I lost all my friends. Rick got caught selling drugs, he had prior convictions and was sent to prison. A dealer befriended me. At least that's what I thought. He became my pimp. Not that I made much money. I had sores over most of my body, weighed less than ninety pounds. I overdosed several times and if it wasn't for Narcan I wouldn't be here."

Joyce pauses.

"Sometimes I felt so worthless I wished I hadn't been saved. I got arrested for theft and possession of meth. The judge sentenced me to drug court and ordered me to live in Serenity House. If I hadn't been arrested, I'd be dead. I wouldn't be here without Serenity House. Without Ellie."

She turns to the director and smiles.

"I've been clean eight months. It hasn't been a straight line. I've relapsed. My parents are back in my life. I'm trying to get my degree and I'm working at a restaurant. I enjoy life again. Learned there is more to life than drugs, drugs, drugs. I've made a few friends who don't use. Every day is still a struggle, but I'm going to make it."

Everyone stands up and claps. Some sob. The director hugs Joyce and she cries.

Why am I so worried people will find out I used? Isn't the important thing that I'm clean? But the outside world still shuns addicts.

Getting clean is way harder than graduating from law school. You have to change your whole way of life. New people, new activities. Addicts have no hobbies. You're one hit away from falling.

Addicts who haven't found recovery resent you. Try to tempt you to use. Law grads look forward to good times. Addicts fear bad times.

Drug dealers ruin people's lives. Some are addicts trying to get money for their next fix. Then there are dealers like Harold in it for the money—don't care who they hurt or kill. And I'm helping Sean keep him in business.

CHAPTER TEN

"Good to see you without your dad."

Frank sits behind his desk, littered with files, pens, coffee cups. Which is more impressive, a cluttered desk or a clean one, with only a phone and computer? Lawyers, no doubt like insurance salesmen, debate this. Frank opts for the clutter, but not by design.

"Yeah, he says hi."

That's good, he's not looking for another lawyer. Maybe Jordan will do what I say. Sean's right, maybe I should buy a more comfortable chair.

Sometimes Frank ushers clients to the small round table in the corner of his office. More informal for wills, adoptions, that sort of thing. But divorce and criminal, he never wants the client to be in control. Clients go postal. He puts them on the other side of his impressive desk, in a chair that's a tad low, and not that comfortable.

"Dad wants me to be a lawyer but he'd end up running my practice like he does everything else. Love to be a doctor but my grades aren't that good."

"Law school is more forgiving. Want a coke? A soft drink? Coffee?"

Jordan shakes his head. "One of my friends says I should go talk to Abby. Tell her how sorry I am."

Shit. I should have warned him before. Malpractice?

"That's the worst thing you can do. Might even be a crime, witness tampering. We can't talk to Abby unless the prosecutor is there. Don't even have your friends try to talk to her. Bad idea."

"But if she knows I'm sorry—"

"Jordan this isn't a high school romance. This is serious shit. Unless you want to go prison, do what I say."

Frank takes a sip of coffee, glad Jordan's chair is uncomfortable.

"Let's talk about your case. It'll come down to who the jurors believe the most. Your lie to the police really hurts us. What hurts them is she was drinking and went into a bedroom to make out with you. Usually juries aren't forgiving but who knows. Some believe all men are Bill Cosby."

"My fraternity had a march in support of #MeToo."

It's amazing how little people know of legal relevance.

"That's nice. Another thing, the doctor's report shows that she wasn't bruised and she didn't tell the cops you forced her into the bedroom. In fact when she got to the rape crisis center she said it might have been her fault."

All of that's good, isn't it." Frank's cell rings, but he turns it off.

Yeah, but I'm worried about Crystal, the girl who told police she was outside the bedroom and heard Abby shouting."

"Crystal's a liar. I used to go out with her, and when I broke it off she said she was going to get even." Frank shakes his head.

"That will help. We can use that to attack her credibility. And it's also improbable she heard Abby cry out and did nothing. Why do you think Abby's saying it was rape?"

"I don't know. Maybe she doesn't want to admit to Crystal or to herself that she was willing. Recalls what actually happened differently."

This guy could make a good lawyer. Or psychiatrist. If he's convicted he'll be lucky to get a job.

"Let's talk about your testimony. When I ask you if you raped Abby, what will you say?"

"That I never forced myself on Abby. I've never forced myself on anyone. With the music, drinking, and making out she wanted it as bad as I did and—"

Frank cuts him off. "Not bad. Two things, don't say Abby wanted it as badly as you did because you don't know that. Say you *thought* she wanted it as badly as you did. Got it?"

"Yes."

Smarter than his dad.

"And don't say you never forced yourself on anyone. If you do, the prosecution can call girls to testify you have."

"But I haven't."

Frank isn't convinced, but maybe. "Best not to get into that fight. Let me explain the weird evidence rule. The state can't bring up prior bad acts unless you open the door by claiming you never did anything wrong. Even if they have girls who claim you forced yourself on them, they can't testify unless you claim you never forced yourself on girls. Even if we could show the girls are lying, best to avoid the fight. Got it?"

"But I've never forced myself on anyone ever."

He still doesn't get it. "I believe you. I just wanted to explain the rule."

"OK."

"When the state questions you they'll go after the lie. Don't try to explain it away, just answer 'yes' or 'no.'The more you say the more trouble you get in. You'll want to explain it, convince the jury it isn't that bad. But don't."

"Got it."

"They'll ask you, one, did you lie to police? Two, did you lie because you were scared? Three, are you scared now? Four, do you lie when you're scared?"

"Shit."

"Just answer yes to each even though you think you can explain things. We'll get to explanations when I question you. Don't worry. We'll go though a trial run before court. Any questions?"

"What should I wear? My dad thinks I should get a new suit for the trial."

I hate to show Paul's incompetent but . . .

"Bad idea. You don't want to come across as a rich fraternity boy. You want to be a regular student, respectful, even humble. When the jurors look at you we want them to see their son, their brother."

"What should I wear? What I wear to school?"

"No, a little more formal: sports jacket, slacks, real shoes. Drop by next week and Cindy will take a look, she has great instincts. Remember the jurors watch you, try to figure you out, so when Abby testifies, don't frown, shake your head. Look at her as someone who has been hurt, who thinks she's a victim, who is mistaken and who is someone you feel badly for."

"I do. I really do."

Most defendants hate their accusers. I like this kid.

"Say hi to your dad."

CHAPTER ELEVEN

Lucy checks the clock on her dash: 4:47 p.m. Shit. The lab closes at 5:00 p.m. They lock the door and if you're not inside you're screwed. Usually Lucy goes after lunch but Frank asked her to write a motion he needs tomorrow, "Can a ten-year-old be sued for injuries he caused by pulling out his grandmother's chair?"

I know family members sometimes hate each other, but this seems ridiculous.

Lucy hates the last-minute emergencies, but that's part of law practice.

I can't be late. If I don't take the test or if I can't pee it's the same as a failure and Character and Fitness won't let me in. For two years I've never missed a test or tested positive. If I don't pee, I won't get a permanent job. I'll get fired.

Shit—a red light. She takes several sips from the extra-large Diet Coke she brought along. Still doesn't feel like peeing.

It's 4:53 p.m. Another red light. More Diet Coke.

Lucy arrives seconds before they close. Signs in, and tries to relax. She finishes her Coke. Still nothing. There's a water fountain in the corner of the room. No cups —they never have cups. Why have a fountain without cups? Nobody has cups in their purse or pocket. She tried to remember to bring a water bottle, but, as usual, she forgot.

The small, shabby waiting room, usually packed, is nearly empty except for a young man and woman who seem to be together. Numerous tats, and piercings. Skinny, jittery, positive. Meth heads.

"Carly."

Carly gets up slowly and follows the tech inside. No way she's looking forward to this. Her friend gives her a thumbs up, puts on his headphones, taps his feet.

Lucy opens her phone to *Apple News.* She can't focus. The tapping doesn't help. She's not going to tell him to stop. Meth heads are dangerous. Lucy wants to get this over with, but the longer she waits, the more likely she'll be able to pee.

"Lucy."

"ID, please." Lucy takes out her license and hands it to a tall, big-boned woman, "Darcy." A new employee? The turnover rate is high. Not surprising. Minimum wage is hardly enough compensation for handling urine, even with gloves. Not to mention dealing with addicts who are often wasted or worse—twitchy, nervous, and angry.

Lucy hands Darcy her jacket, purse, and briefcase. At first she resented them taking her personal stuff, but she knows addicts are always looking for ways to cheat. To figure out a way to have their urine tests, which are positive for heroin, cocaine, or whatever they used, read as clean. There's a whole cottage industry built on beating drug tests. One of the women in her counseling group swore that if you took *Golden Seal* you could test clean. The *whizinator* sells for only $49.95. It's best not described. Cheating doesn't always work. She's heard of people buying urine that turned out to be dirtier than their own.

Darcy hands her a specimen cup. "You have fifteen15 minutes. Not a second more. We're closed. Get here on time. Next time we might not let you in if you pull this. Don't flush and don't wash your hands until you return the jar and I can check the bathroom."

I've heard this at least a hundred times. I'm not a moron, I'm a lawyer—or will be if I can pee. Probably. Why can't they treat us like people? Most of us are trying hard to get clean. I wasn't late.

Lucy closes the door. The staff isn't usually so bitchy, but she's never been here at closing. Maybe Darcy's angry because she'll have to stay late.

The bathroom is plastered with directions on how to take a urine specimen, different instructions for men and women, in

English and Spanish. Now there are new instructions in a language that might be Vietnamese or Arabic. Lucy has read them over and over out of boredom. She wishes she had something else to read. They let men read *Playboy* when they give semen samples. At least, that's what she's heard.

There are ads for various rehab facilities, STD clinics, and other places the administration thinks addicts needs. They're wrong.

The bathroom is the nicest room in the facility: clean, modern, and well-maintained. They must clean the sink and toilet bowl often. Lucy pulls down her pants and underpants and sits on the toilet. She wonders if they have cameras in here? Anywhere but here, peeing isn't a problem. She gets up three or four times a night and rarely gets through a movie without a trip or two to the loo.

Listening to running water helps. She wants to turn on the water in the sink, but she doesn't know if that's allowed. They change the rules all the time without notice to anyone. She doesn't want to take a chance and get into trouble. She taps her feet. Why can't she pee? She thinks about peeing and then tries to not think about peeing.

"Twelve minutes," says Darcy.

She stands and paces the small room. Pushes. A few tiny drops leak out, but not enough.

Calm down Lucy. You have to do this. Your last hurdle. After this you'll never have to put up with this crap. You can do it.

Still nothing.

"Eight minutes."

She pushes and, thank god, this time she has enough to make it to the line on the jar.

She pulls up her clothes and opens the door. Darcy puts on her latex gloves and gingerly takes the cup with a look of distaste on her face. She walks into the bathroom and looks around, in the toilet, in the sink, and in the wastebasket.

"OK, you're done."

Darcy leaves.

She has a tough job. I shouldn't be so hard on her. She's doing her job, might be tired, might have a headache, might be late to pick up her kids. Anyway, I hope I never have to see her again.

CHAPTER TWELVE

Her day starts well. After who knows how long Lucy passes her dental appointment with flying colors, no cavities, no oral cancer, next appointment in six months. The day won't end well.

There are three "call me" notes on her desk, one from Bobby-Jo, the second from her hairdresser, and the third?

Ms. Edwards

Arizona State Bar

480-825-6700

Shit. It's probably to tell me they've turned me down. Would they do that by phone? I have no idea. They would use a woman to break bad news. Or maybe it's to tell me I'm in. Shit, shit, shit.

It's neither. Ms. Edwards tells her that the Character and Fitness Committee wants to meet with her to talk about her application for admission. Would next Thursday at ten work?

Maybe I can put it off a week or so. I'm not ready. But she's not asking me if it will work. I know a summons when I hear one.

This is an important event for the firm as well as for Lucy. Frank and Sean feign casual.

"It could've been worse. They could have told you you're done, adios. Must be they're split," says Sean. "The bad news is Henderson is on the committee. Remember him, Frank? The guy who wanted to send the kid up, what's his name?"

"Arturo. Will Rogers said he never met a man he didn't like; with Henderson he never met a defendant who shouldn't be in prison. But there are good people on the committee. Rumor has it Heather Warren's son died of an overdose and I'm sure everyone on the committee has been touched in some way by drug abuse."

Sean sips his third cup of coffee. "But you don't know how that cuts. Some people become more sympathetic to drug users and others the opposite. Judge Sims's son died of an overdose, but he's the hardest sentencer in drug cases. Thank goodness he can't put first-time users in prison, like he did before the law changed."

"Lucy, it will be fine. Be strong. Don't let them push you around," advises Frank as he glances at the box of donuts Cindy brought. "Be strong. Good advice for me."

The hundred miles of I-10 between Tucson and Phoenix is an ugly drive, even in Cindy's Lincoln. Cindy, bless her, offered it, knowing Lucy's Honda was questionable. The traffic in Phoenix is a bitch. Lucy leaves early after a night of fretful sleep and a great deal of thought of what would be appropriate dress. Too funereal? Too flip?

Will I be asked to make an opening statement? What if I cry? Start to argue? What if they ask about what I had to do to get drugs?

Thanks to the car's GPS she arrives early.

"Your name?" the security officer asks.

"Lucy Wagner."

"Let's see," he consults a list. "Second floor. Conference room."

Lucy sits waiting with two others. Like them she reads, pretends to read, her iPhone. After what seems hours a middle-aged man, walks out, shaking his head, looking down, muttering "Assholes."

Shit. I'm screwed.

"Ms. Wagner."

It's a large, formal, important, scary room. The conference table could seat thirty. On one side sit five lawyers, all dressed professionally, none smiling. Lucy is asked to sit on the other side, facing them.

Don't cry. Should I smile? Act serious?

"Ms. Wagner," begins the African American woman sitting in the middle, "I'm Heather Warren. As you know this committee is considering your application to be admitted to the bar despite your previous drug addiction. You passed the bar exam, were in the top 25 percent, but Character and Fitness held up your admission based on your admitted drug use. We are here to review that decision. Do you have any questions or want to say something before we begin?"

"No."

Why didn't I prepare something? I look stupid.

"We are quite impressed with your submission. Two years of clean drug tests. Many letters telling us what a fine person you are, how you will be a great lawyer. But we know lawyers who have gotten into drugs and have done great harm to their clients. How do we know—no, how do you know you won't relapse?"

Relapse? If this goes badly one hit won't hurt.

"I'll never relapse. I've worked too hard to get here. I've been clean two years and being a lawyer has been my life's dream. When I was an addict I thought I was worthless. Now I love my life. I have a good job. I help others. I try to get enough sleep and eat well."

I'm just rambling. Maybe they don't know that sleep's important.

"If you're overtired or live on sugar that can trigger a relapse. I signed up for a program to go to high and middle schools to talk to kids about drugs."

The man at the end looks up from his files and smiles.

"Ms. Wagner, I'm sure you think you won't relapse. I'm Brad Henderson and I used to work with one of your partners, Frank Perez, wonderful guy."

Shit, is he getting even?

"I know those recovering are convinced they never will. You were in treatment and did well. Do you know how many of the women in rehab with you relapsed?"

Joyce.

"I don't have numbers but relapse is part of recovery."

"I'm sure it is," he nods. "I'm not only worried about relapse. I worry about the message we send to our kids who are considering using drugs. Don't worry, take drugs, you can still be a lawyer."

Be strong, don't let him push you around. Fuck him.

"In recovery the thing that kept most of us going was the notion that we could make it on the outside. Drug addicts think they're worthless. If they're told that even if they kick the habit they'll remain worthless, that's not good. What kept me going was my dream to be a lawyer."

"Last year my son died of an overdose," Heather says. "I hate drugs. How can we prevent wasted lives? Is it better to tell people if you start drugs your life dreams will be crushed and you'll never be what you planned, or help addicts recover by telling them if they get clean they have a future?"

"Telling a kid he'll never be a lawyer, or whatever, if he becomes an addict won't do any good. People experimenting don't think they'll get addicted, it's just one hit."

Henderson drops his friendly pose, "Bob, when I was a prosecutor I heard that crap. Criminals don't think they'll be caught so long sentences don't deter. Damn right they do."

Just sit here. Best thing is when the judges start arguing among themselves. Starving. I'll get a hamburger on my way home.

Henderson and Bob don't seem to like each other; cite studies, personal experiences, counselors, police, and even philosophers. They don't listen to each other and forget Lucy.

What a waste. At least Bob is on my side. How long is this going to go on?

Finally, "Ms. Wagner, we have a lot to discuss. Have a safe drive. We'll let you know."

Jesus, we'll let you know. You might have terminal cancer or all your friends might have been killed. We'll let you know. Check your mail.

The hamburger tastes good, but the drive remains boring.

CHAPTER THIRTEEN

What do you want to be when you grow up?

Sean had to write something, maybe only a paragraph. Probably sixth grade. His dad owned the local hardware store and his mom taught "Special Ed" — kids who became, in a more enlightened time, "Developmentally Disabled." His dad worried about making payroll, paying taxes, and the looming Walmart. Yet, like his mom, he liked going to work. She loved it, she loved "her kids"; most dinners she shared their achievements, their humor, their aliveness. "Danny is reading better, he works so hard."

Sean knew he didn't want to run a hardware store or teach kids, no matter how lovable. So he wrote, "I want to be a lawyer," and went to recess. Kickball was his favorite and he was pretty good. Played baby bunter because he could catch. In high school he gave up his athletic dreams, they didn't play kickball. He became the sports editor on the school newspaper. Played second guitar in a rock group with the unfortunate name, "Thankful Nerds." He was hurt when his friends chose Mickey as first guitar.

In college, even though he was interested in what Sartre had to say, in the mating rituals of hunters and gatherers, and that Shakespeare stole many of his ideas, Sean was seldom inspired and often slept in.

Graduate school was expected but nothing appealed to him. Work? Not yet. He drifted into law school, no noble goal in mind (save the environment), or even an ignoble one (get rich). Maybe juvenile law —at least it would please Mom. But what was supposed to be a three-year reprieve from the real world of work turned into a wonderful intellectual adventure. He never slept in.

In college you discuss free speech, separation of church and state, personal responsibility, and then go get a latte. Those words, those thoughts, become real and vastly more complicated when you have to decide specific cases dealing with hate speech, nativity scenes in public parks, and the criminal responsibility of the mentally ill. Someone wins, someone loses, no one goes to get a latte.

Many of his classmates focused on the justice and fairness of the law, but Sean was fascinated by the process of the law, the critical role facts play in judicial opinions, how judges rely on social science and common sense, how concerned they are in making good law, and how they avoid the rulings in prior cases they don't agree with. At the beginning of *Ghostbusters* Bill Murray said he'd never have sex with a ghost. Then he met a beautiful ghost. That wasn't a rule. He figured it was more of a guideline.

Sean wasn't concerned about grades and had never heard of Law Review. When first year grades came out he was pleasantly surprised and bought a six-pack of Pabst to celebrate with Harriet, the woman he had married shortly before law school.

"Great. When you graduate you can get a job at a big firm and we can move to Phoenix or LA."

Beer and Harriet, two mistakes, but only one he had to live with. He divorced second year.

After graduation he took a job in juvenile court. His mother was thrilled. Harriet would've been pissed.

"Sean, your dad and I are so proud. You could have gone with a big LA firm but instead juvenile court. You'll be able to help."

Fat chance.

After a year Sean became disillusioned. He knew that early last century juvenile court was a great reform, a place to keep troubled kids out of adult prison, to teach them skills, convince them that they could succeed. In the real world he learned that a wonderful dream often stays a dream: too few good foster homes, too little money for programs, and too many drugs on the street and in juvie.

He decided to go into private practice with Frank. Whose name went first was decided by a coin flip. Sean failed to convince Frank that he meant two out of three.

He enjoys private practice, likes many of the clients and learning new law. The firm has great people, Frank, Cindy, the new girl, and Dusty. Poor Dusty had to stay home when he worked at juvie. But Sean is still not sure if law is the life for him.

Take today. He's going to court to try to get a drug dealer off. Sure, everyone's entitled to a lawyer, that's noble, but if he wins he won't be phoning home.

Maybe I should have stayed at juvie. Call it quits when you can't help everyone? Mom didn't call it quits. Maybe I should have been a teacher, gone into the Peace Corps, joined the army, or helped friends find the right hammer.

Department 17, Superior Court.

Judge Weaver: This is the time for the defendant's motion to exclude the evidence found at 910 Randlett. Are you ready to proceed?

Sean: Yes, Your Honor.

DA White: Yes.

Judge: It's your motion, Mr. O'Grady, proceed.

Sean: The police had absolutely no reason to suspect that house contained illegal drugs. Since 1965 and the case of Mapp v. Ohio, a search of a house without a valid warrant is a violation of the Fourth Amendment and any evidence they seize cannot be used at trial, the fruit of the poisonous tree.

Judge: Get to it, O'Grady, don't waste my time. I've been to law school. There's a warrant, approved by a neutral judge. Reliable informant, good description of location and what is to be seized. So what's the problem?

Sean: It's our position that the warrant was invalid because police obtained it by lying to the informant.

DA White: Excuse me, Your Honor, this is ridiculous. Police lie to defendants all the time and no court has said that's wrong.

Sean: This isn't your co-defendant confessed and says you had the gun. In this case, the informant, a Mexican, was told by the police that unless he gave up the stash house, they would turn him over to ICE to be deported. He explained he has papers, has worked in this country for twenty-three years, and has a wife and two children, both citizens, ages eight and twelve. The police told him they have friends at ICE, that ICE makes mistakes, that before the week was up he would be deep in Mexico and probably would never see his family again.

Judge: Do you have any cases where a court threw out a search warrant due to police bad behavior?

Sean: Yes, while it's not directly on point, Mapp v. Ohio. The Supreme Court ruled that the only way to prevent illegal police activity is to deny them the fruit of that activity by suppressing the evidence they seized.

DA White: Mapp doesn't apply. In that case there was a clear Constitutional violation, a search of a house without a warrant, and in this case at most there was only some bad behavior. If the court adopts the defendant's argument the courts will have to decide exactly what the police can and cannot do and there is no standard.

Sean: As to the lack of a clear definition, in a Supreme Court case dealing with pornography, it was argued you can't outlaw pornography because you can't define it. Justice Stewart said, "You know it when you see it." You know what the cops did here was wrong and just because there might be close cases doesn't mean you don't act on the clear ones.

Judge: Mr. White?

DA White: You still face the lack of a standard problem. Police won't know what they can do. If there are abuses the police department should correct them, not the courts.

Sean: You can't expect police to police themselves.

Judge: I'll take this under advisement. Bailiff, call the next case.

Back at the firm Sean stops at the new girl's office. She had helped him prepare his argument.

"It went well. Thanks for coming up with 'you know it when you see it.' It might have saved the day."

"Thanks for the compliment. But I'm not happy helping put a drug dealer back on the street."

"We won't be doing that. The law will be doing that. Got time for a latte?"

Lucy accepts. A chance to know Sean better and keep her mind off her interview with the friendly folks on the Character and Fitness committee.

Home, she pets Teddy, fills his water bowl. Straightens up the debris on the kitchen table. Pays a couple bills. When she can hold out no longer, she checks the mail. Her heart begins to pound. She wants the letter from the bar, but no news is good news. She thinks she has a good chance of being admitted. At least she did before her interview.

At times she's sure she'll get in, be a lawyer, get a permanent job. But the next day, or the next hour, or the next thought, she's sure she'll be rejected. No one promised her she would pass if she had two years clean. Maybe the lawyers on the committee want to prove how tough they are. Maybe they're sick of what the opioid epidemic has done to the legal profession.

One wonderful hit never hurt anyone.

Nothing compares to that feeling when the drugs start to flow through your bloodstream. You don't have to worry about how you look, becoming a lawyer, or relationships. Everything is fine. Everything is terrific.

Until the next day.

When she gets the letter she's afraid to open it. If they say no, she's toast. She's done everything they asked of her. A "no" could tip the scales. Forget being a lawyer. She opens it.

"We are pleased to inform you . . ."

She rereads it, once, twice.

I'm a lawyer. Who should I call first? Clay, Ethel, Bobby-Jo, Frank, Sean? Maybe a permanent job. No more humiliation. No more excuses when someone asks why I'm not a lawyer. No more drug tests. No more peeing.

"Teddy, come here I'm a lawyer." Teddy cocks his head. Wags his tail.

CHAPTER FOURTEEN

To celebrate Lucy being a lawyer Frank and Sean take her to Taco Giro for lunch.

"This place is terrific," says Frank, "unless there's Mariachi music."

"Frank, us Irish love Mariachi music."

"No, you Irish love beer. Two Irish guys walk out of a pub." Frank stops, says nothing, Sean and Lucy look puzzled, shrug.

After a few moments Frank smiles, "It's possible."

Salsa, hot and mild, is on the table. The waitress brings drinks, beer for Sean and iced tea for Frank and Lucy. Sean raises his glass, "To the newest member of the Arizona State Bar!"

"Bravo," echoes Frank. "Now we can give you some trials."

"Are you ready to order?"

"I'll have a number five." Sean always orders the taco, tamale, and enchilada plate. He remembers his childhood visits to his aunts in Santa Barbara, the beach, the music, the cascarones, but mostly the tacos, tamales, and enchiladas. Lucy chooses a chicken topopo salad and Frank fish tacos.

Trials. I hated the two I did in law school. I always hated talking in front of other people, but trials are worse. Someone sitting at the next table, ready to pounce on you if you make a mistake. Objections on grounds you never heard of. The judge expecting you to say something.

"I'm not ready."

"Sure you are. We'll second chair you," Frank says as he dips a chip into the salsa. "I have a domestic violence case coming up. I represent the husband. It'll look good to have a woman represent him."

"I'll have to argue it was the wife's fault?"

"Lucy," Frank says, "maybe it was. Domestic violence isn't always black and white. Hear what your client has to say. If it goes to trial, you'll present his side. If the jury doesn't buy it, you'll lose. But don't worry, the case might go away. Probably she'll refuse to testify. Once he apologizes, sends flower, and promises not to do it again, she'll realize she still loves him."

"And," Sean adds, "if there's a kid, she'll need the income. And speaking of dismissals, the DA is dismissing the case against our favorite drug dealer, Harold."

"The judge bought your argument about police lying to get a search warrant?"

"They dismissed before Weaver could rule. She's a loose cannon. They're worried she might rule cops can't lie to get a search warrant. That would be a terrible precedent for them. Gives defense lawyers another way to attack."

"Why didn't you tell me, Sean? That's a real win for us."

"I only got the call a few minutes before we left for lunch."

Frank looks at him and shakes his head.

I can't just sit here. I need them to understand the harm Harold does. What it's like to be ruled by drugs, how hard rehab is. About Joyce and the women at Serenity. About sleazy dealers demanding sex.

"What about Harold's victims? Thanks to folks like him I almost ruined my life. I didn't spend three years in law school learning how to get him back on the street."

"Calm down, Lucy," responds Sean. "Yeah, I worry about that some. But I wasn't defending Harold, I was defending the Constitution. Do we want cops threatening to illegally deport Mexicans unless they do what they want?"

"You realize the correct word is Latinos?" says Frank.

"Latinos, Hispanics, Chicanos—it's hard to keep up."

"Sometimes police just know someone's guilty and they step over the line to get them. When I was a DA I had to tell them I wouldn't prosecute a case if they stopped the car without cause, searched a house without a warrant, or were too rough questioning a defendant. They were pissed but became better cops."

The waitress returns, hands the salad to the señorita, the tacos to Frank, and the number five to Sean, warning him "the plate is hot." Has anyone sued over a hot plate, spilled tacos? Should they require a waiver?

They fall silent. Sean is lost in thought.

"I worry about Harold. He's a jerk," says Sean. "A few months ago I won a drunk driving case and the next week the guy drives drunk and kills a young woman. I blamed the cops for not doing a better job investigating the case and the prosecutor for not doing a better job, but I know the reason he was back on the street is because I'm a better lawyer."

"Sean, you're not that good. You can't throw cases. Lucy, we're not planning to be a drug firm but until we get more in the black we have to represent anyone who walks in."

I shouldn't have admitted I'm afraid to do trials. That I don't want to represent drug dealers or men in domestic violence cases. Lowest person on the totem pole can't be choosy. I might have blown it, never get a permanent job. I need to act tougher even if I'm not.

"Look guys, I know we have to do all we can for our clients."

"Frank, she did a great job helping me on Harold's motion even if she's not a fan."

"And I'll do trials. I have great teachers. I like working with you guys. And Cindy and Dusty are great."

"They are."

"Where did you get Dusty?"

"In my previous life I was married for a short bit. Very short. When I got a divorce we argued over Dusty, even though she never seemed to care about him. Complained he shed on the furniture. Chewed shoes. Jumped on the bed. She settled for the forty-inch TV."

I wonder why he never mentioned being married before. Of course, I've only been here a short time.

Sean signals the waitress. “I'll have another beer, I'm Irish. Lucy, I hear you and Clay Blake are an item.”

Embarrassed but relieved, she thinks perhaps she's one of the boys, “Where'd you hear that?”

For a moment Sean smiles.

Did Cindy tell? She wouldn't do that, would she?

“I saw you two having breakfast at Baja Sunday morning. You had that just-got-out-of-bed look.”

Lucy blushes.

Frank, taking pity, changes the subject. “Speaking of getting rich, we're doing OK, but we should consider advertising. Maybe TV.”

Sean spills salsa on his sport coat. What if it stains? Lawsuit. Does the restaurant have a duty to serve nonstaining salsa?

“Great to advertise, NFL games. We'll need a slogan. A guy in California used, ‘Reasonable Doubt at a Reasonable Price.’ We'll have a picture of the four of us, looking tough.”

“Four?” asks Lucy.

“Cindy has to be in it. Dressed inappropriately.”

“Men are disgusting.” Lucy shakes her head but smiles.

“Lucy, it's NFL football. Flesh is mandatory. And us men aren't disgusting. It's just we see all those Viagra ads and wonder what we're missing.”

It's a lot like lunch with the public defenders.

CHAPTER FIFTEEN

Ethel has jury duty, which gives Lucy and her sister an excuse to have lunch. They rarely eat lunch together because Ethel hates driving downtown and Lucy doesn't have time to meet elsewhere. Lucy picked Cafe 54, which has a menu good enough for her picky sister, and is close to court. She goes there often. It's staffed by people with mental health problems who are training for food service jobs.

The food is delicious, the restaurant dingy. The tables don't match and you have to order at the counter. Instead of a number you're given a placard with the name and short bio of someone who suffers from a mental illness. Folks like Michael Phelps, Terry Bradshaw, Miley Cyrus, and Emma Stone.

If celebrities can admit they have mental health problems, maybe someday I can admit I was an addict. If they add addicted folks to the placards they'll never run out.

Ethel arrives a few moments after Lucy. "Congratulations, counselor." She hugs her tight. She looks around. "Are you sure the food is good here. It looks like a dump."

"Yes, give it a chance, Sis." Ethel spends several minutes looking at the menu. Lucy hopes she won't ask her numerous questions about the food. Is it organic? Antibiotic free? Produced locally? She doesn't. Lucy chooses a curry chicken salad with pieces of pineapple and mango and after much thought Ethel orders the Korean Bulgogi Bowl. Ethel pays no attention to the Ellen DeGeneres placard.

"How's jury duty? You on a case?" Ethel nods. "Tell me about it."

"Am I allowed to? The judge said not to talk about it."

"Anything that's public record. Name of the judge, lawyers, what he's charged with."

"Some guy who couldn't have a gun had one. Felon in possession of a weapon? I think that's what Judge Brooks said. She's impressive. The defense attorney's last name is Cardenas, don't remember the prosecutor's, but they're all women."

Lucy smiles. "I'd love to be on a jury. When it's over, I want to hear all about it."

The server, a man with Down Syndrome, could have been any age from twenty to forty. He brings their food and offers a roll. "Need anything else?" He says, each word slowly. They shake their heads, no. For a minute there's only chewing.

"So how's it going with Clay?"

"Too good. He's kind and sweet. I've never been treated so well. I keep thinking he'll end it."

"Why? Don't give me the I'm a fat drug addict crap. You've lost weight, you're clean, and Sis, you're right, this food is delicious. How do I get more iced tea?"

"Told ya it would be." Lucy takes the glasses, fills them, and returns.

"What's he done that makes you think he's going to end it?"

"Nothing, it's all me. I mess up everything."

"You've got to change your attitude."

"I know."

"What about work? They must be glad you're a 'real' lawyer."

Lucy ignores her jab. "So far, so good. No permanent offer."

"When they know how good you are you'll be in."

Oh shit, the office meeting.

She looks at her phone, checks the time. "I've got to go in ten minutes and you need to get going. Judges don't look kindly on jurors being late, especially federal judges with life tenure."

Friday afternoon office meeting. They're sitting in the firm's library and conference room, which used to be a kitchen. Table for six, some desert landscapes on the wall, bookshelves filled with law books the firm bought from a solo practitioner who was hanging it up. No one uses books anymore, they're there to impress clients. And of course there's everyone's favorite painting, *Dogs playing Poker*.

It's been a tough week and everyone is a tad tired. Except Dusty, who never is—or always is. There's bagels and cream cheese, munchies, beer, cokes, a pot of fresh coffee, and bad jokes. Updates on pending cases.

"Lucy, what did you find out on the Morgan divorce?"

An old lawyer's adage: "Criminal law you see bad people at their best; family law you see good people at their worst." Divorces often come down to accusations, name-calling, and money. Ms. Morgan and her (expletive deleted) husband are fighting over custody of their son and, of course, money. In the heat of battle, priorities get muddled. A family court judge once told Frank, "If either party stops talking about what a terrible person their spouse is, and at least mentions their kids, that person wins."

Frank had asked Lucy to research a community property issue. How is a settlement from a husband's accident split up? If it's community property it's split equally between the wife and husband. If it isn't community property, he could keep it all. Confident he would never do divorce work, which he ended up doing, he didn't take the course. Lucy did; it was scheduled midmorning, taught by a prof with a good reputation.

The class was invigorating, strong opinions and insights on all sides. Is it a good idea for parents to adopt a disabled child when they have children who aren't? Does "no fault" divorce, besides wrecking the private detective industry, tend to undermine the seriousness of marriage and thus harm children? And what about "palimony"—allowing unwed partners to get financial support when they split. The famous case was against Lee Marvin, the gunslinger in *Cat Ballou*. He won on the screen, but lost in court.

Law profs love big questions, not small statutes, the bread and butter of law practice. "I found a statute on point. The amount awarded for pain and suffering is his to keep, the rest for lost wages and things like that, is community property and our client should get half."

"Kick ass, Lucy. Write a memo for the file. Let's talk about jury selection. Jordan's trial is coming up."

Some claim the right jury is game over. There are for-hire "jury consultants" who arrogantly claim people are open books and cynically suggest they're incapable of changing their minds. But in the push and pull of a courtroom you never can tell. Trial lawyers tell of jurors who they just knew were against them who ended up saving them . . . and, after a few drinks, vice versa.

While your goal may be to get jurors who'll be with you at the end of the trial, good luck with that. The best you can hope for are jurors who are on your side at the start. Jurors leaning pro prosecution will tend to see the evidence that way; those pro defense will see other things. More likely than not, they'll be with you at the end.

"Get old folks on the jury. They don't realize that girls go to parties, drink, flirt, and make out. They won't like Abby."

"Sean, what if they have granddaughters?" Lucy smiles. "If I were the prosecutor I'd try to get jurors who resent fraternities, maybe men who haven't gone to college."

"Or maybe guys like me who didn't get in," Sean laughs. "Of course I wouldn't want to be in a fraternity that would let me in."

"Old joke, Sean, no wonder they didn't choose you. I'm going to keep off #MeToo women."

"I read Jordan's interview," Lucy runs her fingers though her hair. "He said his frat had a march in support of the movement. Big deal."

"I'm not going to touch that," nods Frank. "If I ask Jordan about #MeToo I'll open the door for the prosecution to get into things better left out. 'Jordan, you do realize that it takes real courage to come forward after being sexually abused because so many refuse to believe truthful women?' No thanks."

And on it goes. None of this ends with a checklist, a "do or don't" list, but it sharpens one's intuition for the critical moment when the judge asks, "Mr. Perez, do you pass the panel?"

CHAPTER SIXTEEN

The last time she saw her mother alive Lucy was rushing to beat the morning bell at Tucson High. Her mom lay on the couch covered by a ragged blanket watching a sitcom rerun on cable. Since her terminal diagnosis that was what she did. No rage, rage, against the dying of the light, it was "Change the channel."

Lucy's on her way to see a client at hospice. Someone who's dying. She can't stop thinking about her mom.

I knew she was dying, so did she. Why didn't we talk about it? Tell her I'll be with her, she won't be alone. Tell her I was afraid of what would happen to me.

She's relieved when she walks into St. Judes. It doesn't reek of disinfectants, sorrow, and death. It's a free-standing building, tasteful blue corridors, welcoming nurses, and, in one room, a woman playing a harp for the patient and her family. It's hard not to glance into the rooms, some filled with relatives, talking, holding the patient's hand, other rooms empty but for a bed, a white sheet, and someone sleeping. TVs, few with sound, play in every room.

She finds Mary Smith, her client, in Room C8, sitting up in bed wearing baby-blue old-fashioned pajamas like the ones her grandma wore. Next to her sits a woman in her sixties, who gives the impression she's trying to look fashionable, but doesn't. Her dyed blond hair too brassy, her silver-rimmed glasses too large. Her lime green tunic designed for a much younger person and when she stands it's obvious her skin-tight gray leggings do nothing for her oversized rear end. Both her blue eye makeup and dark red lipstick are smeared.

"Hi, Ms. Smith, I'm Lucy Wagner, the lawyer you called. Nice to meet you in person. Call me Lucy." No way would she feel comfortable with a woman three times her age calling her Ms. Wagner.

"OK, Lucy, thanks for coming. A woman lawyer! Good for you, my, how things change."

"For the better. We're making progress."

Mary is energized, remembering. "In elementary school I argued so well people told me I should be a lawyer."

"I'm sure, Mary, you did more good as a teacher than as a lawyer. I remember my third grade teacher, Mr. Davis. Told me I could do better. Go to college. Changed my life."

"But the pay is better. And having women lawyers, doctors, is so much better. If I had a granddaughter I'd tell her to be president. I always knew we were smarter. This is Roberta, my caregiver and friend. She's wonderful. I want to leave everything to her."

Roberta forces a cold smile and Lucy immediately dislikes her.

Lucy wants to specialize in elder law. She'll have to get more comfortable with end of life. A hospice nurse came to their Elder Law class and said working with the dying is the most meaningful thing she has done. She is now comfortable with death.

I'll help people in hard times, people like my mother. I won't have to go to trial or deal with the likes of Harold.

"So you want to change your will?"

"Change my beneficiary from my son, Gerald, to Roberta."

Shit. Elder law isn't only smiling elderly couples setting up educational trusts for their grandchildren. Sometimes it's the stuff of human drama.

"Well, before we can talk Roberta will have to leave the room."

"Why? I want her to stay."

"Sorry, can't be done. If she's the beneficiary the law requires she leave the room." Lucy is glad this is the legal rule. She isn't sure about Roberta but knows abusers never want their victim to be alone with their friends and family.

Roberta forces another cold smile, and gives Mary a quick hug. "I'll be here if you need me, dear." She glares at Lucy. "Hope it won't be long."

Does Mary have legal capacity? Bizarre deathbed requests are always open to challenge and the son might not be too happy. Lucy runs through the traditional questions to test competence, "If you were planning a trip to New York how would you get there?" Trouble if the answer is "I don't know" or if they end up in Nova Scotia.

Mary has a pretty good grasp on things, at least on getting to New York. But given that a will contest is probable, Lucy decides she should have a doctor examine her.

"Why do you want to change your will?"

"I want to give Roberta everything." Mary pauses, frowns. "Gerald is a homo."

A homo? Lucy's shocked. She hadn't heard that word in ages.

"How do you know he's gay?"

"Gay? Political correctness. He's queer. Roberta told me."

Lucy looks down, remembers Mel, freezes.

Cut out her son because he's gay. No way. I need to talk to the guys.

"Do you have a copy of your will?"

"No, but Roberta wouldn't mind getting it for me."

"OK, I'll need to read it to begin working, figure out my fee. How about I come back tomorrow afternoon around two?"

Driving back she thinks of Mel. In high school she was his cover girlfriend; he ate lunch with her, took her to the prom, mentioned she had a great ass. Only fooled the boys. Died of AIDS. Funniest man she ever knew. Told great gay jokes, planned to be an actor. If he'd only been straight she might've married him.

Can I represent a woman who wants to disinherit her son because he's gay? Mel would have something funny to say but I don't. Take the moral high ground and lose one of my few clients? I criticized Sean about Harold. Maybe I can talk Mary out of it. Roberta's a smug bitch. Shit.

CHAPTER SEVENTEEN

Lucy works late. Leaves worked exhausted. She plans to go home, eat a *Lean Cuisine* and go to sleep, alone. She adores Clay, but staying healthy and getting enough sleep matters.

One wonderful hit never hurt anyone.

Clay likes to stay up late. They're still new to each other and talk for hours—if they aren't making love. She'd just finished eating when Clay calls, "Any chance you can come by? Feels like days since I've seen you."

Usually they sleep at her house, otherwise she has to lug her makeup, hair dryer, clothes, and face creams to his place. Almost fills a small suitcase. Clay only needs a toothbrush. And she has to leave Teddy home alone. Clay's building doesn't allow pets. In spite of these annoyances, Lucy agrees. She spends a few minutes fussing over Teddy. Promises him a long walk then takes off.

I should've suggested he come to my house, told him I'm too tired to go out. But what if he thinks that's an excuse? If I tell him the truth—that recovering addicts need their sleep—that will be the end.

When she arrives Clay is watching baseball. She sits next to him on the couch and falls asleep. Somehow she wound up in the bedroom, and got undressed, but she doesn't remember anything after sitting on the couch.

The alarm rings. Clay wakes up wide awake. Lucy groans. "Come on, Lucy, time to get up. It's a workday." They talk and kiss for a few minutes. Clay looks at the clock. "I better get moving. Mind if I shower first? I'll be fast."

Lucy nods.

Clay's phone is charging on the nightstand. She grabs it. She isn't sure why. Maybe it's her damn insecurity. Why would a cute, smart guy like Clay pick her?

She scans recent calls. Mostly from her, a couple from his brother, and two from Carla. Whose Carla? Jealousy. She goes to voicemail. Hits Carla's call. "Hi, Clay. Wanted to tell you I left Super Cuts and I'm working at Hair on Broadway—"

She freezes halfway through the call. The shower is no longer running. She looks up to see Clay still wet, staring.

"What the fuck are you doing?"

What can I say? I could tell him I'm making a call, but he'll never believe me. My phone is next to the bed fully charged. There's nothing to say.

"I'm sorry Clay."

"Have I ever given you one reason to think I lie or cheat?"

"No."

"We never agreed to any kind of commitment, but if you know me at all, you know I'm not that kind of guy."

Don't cry. Men hate that. Have I ruined our relationship?

"No, Clay. You've been great. It's me. I'm not good at trusting people."

"Spying on them isn't going to help."

He grabs his pants, shirt, and a tie. Leaves the bedroom. Lucy sits on the bed.

I'm so stupid.

She doesn't want to shower in case he wants to talk. The minutes pass. Lucy realizes she might be late if she doesn't start getting ready.

"I'm going to work. Let yourself out," says Clay.

"Clay, I'm sorry." He slams the front door. Tears fall freely. After a few minutes, she pulls herself together, showers and dresses.

Lucy parks her Honda as close to the office as possible, even though there's only a two-hour meter. No quarters—she'll have to use her debit card and waste more time. It's 8:11 a.m. She's never been told to show up at 8:00 a.m. but that's when the office opens, when Cindy gets there.

I'm such a friggin' idiot. I've just ruined the best relationship I've ever had.

She walks into the office and is greeted by the odor of fresh coffee. It's quiet. Maybe Frank and Sean aren't in yet. And where's Dusty? Cindy is staring into space.

"Good morning." Cindy's always cheerful voice is flat.

"Morning, Cindy."

"Lucy, something the matter, you OK? Looks like you've been crying."

"No, I'm fine. Got some mascara in my eye."

Oh god, I wish she hadn't noticed.

"Are you sure you're OK?"

"Yes, I'm sure."

"Come get a cup of coffee with me. I just brewed a batch," Cindy says.

"OK," says Lucy although she'd rather be alone and think about what happened with Clay.

They go into the conference room. Cindy pours two cups of coffee and sits down at the table. "Have a seat."

"I have work to do."

"Just for a few minutes—I need to talk to you."

I sit down. What's with her?

"You got a strange call this morning." Cindy checks the message.

"Strange call?"

"Do you know a woman named Joyce?"

"Yes."

"Are you close?"

Shit. Why does she want to know? If I say we're close Cindy might ask how I know her. I can't tell her we went through rehab together.

"Not really."

"A Mrs. Rosenblatt, Ellie, called to tell you that Joyce passed away."

Joyce? Dead?

Lucy turns white.

"Sit down. I'll get you some water."

Lucy sits. Dusty, who'd been in his bed, walks over, puts his head on her knee. She pets him, feeling calmer.

"Can I get you something else to drink? If you need to take some time for yourself I'll tell the guys. They'll understand."

"Thanks, Cindy, I'll be fine," Lucy gets up muttering as she walks into her office. Closes the door.

Joyce, dead. How? Did she OD? She was doing so great. Her speech. When she first arrived at Serenity she was a complete mess—skinny, arms and legs full of sores, looked like she hadn't slept in months. Joking around. She'd relapsed over and over, but never lost her sense of humor.

One wonderful hit never hurt anyone.

CHAPTER EIGHTEEN

No way can she stay in the office. She doesn't want to break down in front of the guys or Cindy. She needs to figure out what happened to Joyce or maybe it could happen to her. And how to fix things with Clay?

Lucy throws a couple case files into the car and drives to a Starbucks out of downtown. There are two or three better coffee shops within walking distance of the firm, but the last thing she wants is to see anyone she knows, especially anyone from the PD. Thanks to her desire to impress Clay, her diet has been a success. Today, she can treat herself to whatever she wants. Better calories than drugs. She orders a vanilla latte and classic coffee cake.

She needs to apologize. But how? No way is she going to his office. She couldn't bear it if Clay treated her badly in front of her colleagues. He's not the type to yell or call her names, but she couldn't take him being cold. Email is too impersonal, too cowardly. Maybe the phone? She should ask Bobby-Jo for advice. She needs to talk to her about Joyce. Poor Joyce.

What's wrong with me? I'm obsessing over a fight with my boyfriend and Joyce is dead.

She dials Bobby-Jo, "If you're looking for Bobby-Jo, leave your name, number, a brief message, and you might get lucky."

Her voice makes Lucy feel better.

Bobby-Jo and Lucy have become close friends. Their relationship was kind of lopsided in the beginning. Lucy came to Bobby-Jo for help. They drank hundreds of cups of coffee while Lucy talked about her life and problems. Only recently had Bobby-Jo started to talk about herself.

Lucy and her only sister, Ethel, no brothers, were born in Tucson to middle-class parents. Their financial situation worsened when their dad died. Between his life insurance and their mom's job they always had enough to eat and go to a cheap restaurant once a month. As a child she never worried about money.

Bobby-Jo's life was different. She was born in the Bible Belt, the oldest of six kids. Her father who had been a janitor and church deacon died when the youngest was five. Her mother worked two jobs: nights as a cashier at a convenience store and the morning shift at the neighborhood elementary school feeding free breakfasts to hungry kids. Being the oldest, Bobby-Jo was expected to take care of her brothers and sisters. Her mother also expected her to go to church, finish high school, and marry a nice Baptist boy.

Life was tough. Bobby-Jo's mother didn't make enough to feed and clothe five kids. Some nights they went to bed hungry.

Lucy can't imagine being hungry. Dieting is one thing—a thing you choose—but a kid who has to go to bed without supper . . .

Growing up, the refrigerator was always full. She'd never missed a meal nor had anyone she knew.

At first Lucy wasn't sure about Bobby-Jo. She was warm with a great sense of humor, but she was forty-one, fifteen years older than her, and a lesbian. Would Bobby-Jo understand her problems?

So what if she's gay? Mel understood my problems. Even in high school.

Once she got to know Bobby-Jo she realized lesbians had the same problems as everyone else, relationships, jobs, self-doubt, and the call of drugs.

Lucy's phone rings. It's Bobby-Jo. "Lucy, something the matter, hon?"

"Yes, it's been a terrible day. Hold on a sec, I'm at Starbucks. I'm going to sit outside so I can hear you." Lucy grabs her stuff and moves outside to one of the covered tables. No one else is out there.

"Mine, too. I guess you heard about Joyce?" asks Bobby-Jo.

"What happened, do you know?"

"Nobody had seen Joyce for a day or so. Didn't answer her cell. She didn't show up for a group she led and that night missed dinner at her parents'. Her mom went to her house and found her in the bathroom. Laying on the floor, a needle in her arm."

"How horrible for her mom. Suicide or overdose?"

Suicide? It's common with us druggies.

"Too early to say." Both fall silent.

"Joyce seemed so together at the lunch," Lucy breaks the silence. "Her speech was terrific. People at my table cried."

"That lunch is a curse. This is the second year in a row one of the speakers died."

One wonderful hit never hurt anyone.

They talk about Joyce but worry about themselves.

"I'm scared," Lucy says.

"So am I. Time helps, but I'm never sure I'll be clean forever. Whenever someone falls off the wagon, I think I'll be next. I want a drink—several drinks."

"Me too. Clay and I had a fight this morning."

"That's one thing us dykes don't have to worry about—boyfriends. It's always good to apologize even if it's their fault. It usually is."

"It was my fault."

"Have you apologized?"

"Not yet. I can't show up at his job. I used to work there. It'd be so embarrassing if he's still angry. I thought about calling to apologize and suggest we get together and talk."

"Good idea, but he may not be ready yet. Give him some time to calm down."

"OK."

"Do you want to go out tonight, have dinner?"

Lucy is quiet.

"I get it. You want to see him. Hang around in case he calls. You need to be more independent." Bobby-Jo sighs. "I'll check in on you later. Promise you'll stay clean till we talk."

"One day at a time. I will. Promise."

"Call me anytime if you need me."

Lucy finishes her coffee cake. She wants something else sweet. No, she's had one treat.

I'm not going to use Joyce's death or Clay being angry as an excuse to eat. Bobby-Jo's right about waiting. But I can't. I'm too anxious. I have to try and fix it. Now.

Opening her phone, she drafts a text.

Clay, I'm sorry. I had no business looking at your phone. Please call me. Let's get together and talk about it. I have trust issues. I know that. I've made mistakes in the past. I'll get better. Give me another chance.

Lucy rereads and deletes. She sounds desperate and it's way too long. She's not writing *Anna Karenina*.

She tries again.

Sorry. I was out of line. Hope you can forgive me.

She's not sure about this one either. Screw it. She pushes send.

CHAPTER NINETEEN

It's raining cats and dogs. Sorry Dusty. Hot, over 100 degrees, sudden high winds, gathering dark clouds, hard, driving rain, dropping temperatures, loud thunder claps, lightning, dogs whining. Then, all is quiet.

Frank's suit jacket is soaked, the monsoon unexpected. Entering the firm's library, "It's good for the crops."

"What crops? We live in the desert." Sean sits at the conference table and looks up from his computer, files in neat piles. Lucy sits across from him with her computer, files a mess.

"Come on, Sean, didn't you learn Arizona's big three C's? Copper, Cotton, and . . . I forget the third," Frank admits.

"Senility."

"That doesn't start with a C . . . if I remember correctly."

Lucy knows there are five C's: Copper, Cotton, Cattle, Citrus, hmmm, can't remember the fifth, keeps her mouth shut. Knowing more than the bosses, not a good plan.

Friday afternoon office meeting, time to catch up, talk law, and have a brew. It's the usual suspects: Frank, Sean, Lucy, and the sleeping Dusty. Warm greetings, they like each other.

Frank, now in shirtsleeves, sits. "I just came from Richmond's office. We've finally settled the Morgan case. Beginning to think they would die first. We'll be getting a large fee."

"Divorces aren't worth it." Sean is wearing his "no court Friday outfit," jeans and a red polo emboldened with a large blue "Arizona." He has one of the most valued things in Tucson, season tickets to Wildcat basketball. "Remember my Atwater case? Joint custody of the kids. Third time this month, twice on the weekend, my client calls and screams that her two-timing ex-husband brought the kids home ten minutes late. Wants me to get him thrown in jail."

Frank turns to Lucy. "Today's lesson—never give clients your home number. Besides the wonderful world of family law, what's up, Sean?"

"Last week I was in the court of your law school pal, Manny Mejias. One day a week he turns his court into Veterans Treatment court. Vets can get minor criminal matters dismissed if they go to the VA for treatment for PTSD, drugs, that sort of thing."

"Manny was always a very creative guy. I've heard great things about the court. In a couple of years, more than five hundred homeless vets off the streets and most have jobs."

"Talked me into spending a couple of afternoons a month supervising the law students who represent the vets. Might learn something."

"That's Manny. He had us out registering voters instead of studying. Lucy? Anything new on the hospice front?"

"The client hired me to rewrite her will, but I need advice."

"Lucy, you're the expert. You took Elder Law. We took Corporations, dreaming of top-floor corner offices with very tasteful abstracts on the walls, not *Dogs Playing Poker*."

Sean adds, "And they have martinis instead of cheap beer. So, Luce, what's the problem?"

"The client wants me to redo her will, cut out her son and leave everything to her caregiver."

"Why?" Frank asks.

"Her son's gay. Her caregiver told her."

Sean walks to the end of the table and, seeing there is no other option, takes the last IPA. "Is he gay? We can always send Cindy to find out."

Lucy, despite herself, smiles. "Men are disgusting."

"Sean, lemonade for you next week," Frank shakes his head.

Dusty, nap over, walks under the table looking for a sympathetic hand. Waddled over would be more accurate. Lucy, concerned and something of an expert, says, "Dusty's getting fat."

Sean rushes to Dusty's defense, "He's doing great, measured in dog pounds." No smiles. You can't win them all. "Seriously, even if he is gay that's no reason to disinherit him. Talk her out of it. Tell her how much pain that will inflict."

"I'm not sure it's our job to talk clients out of what they want," Frank says. "What we need to do is to force them to think deeper. Sean, remember Professor Binder?"

"Yeah, his famous hypo: your client wants to pave paradise and put in a parking lot. What do you do?"

Frank nods. "Half my class said, 'Do it. If you don't the guy down the street will, and it's his decision, we're hired guns.' The other half pretty much argued the first half was immoral. After a good half hour and a lot of hurt feelings the professor said both sides were wrong. Lucy, did you take his class?"

"No, took Bergman's. All we talked about was whether corporate lawyers represent the corporation, the board, individual board members, the CEO, or various secretaries and janitors. He had a hypo where they all sued each other."

"Did you learn anything?"

"Not to be a corporate lawyer," says Lucy. "What about paradise?"

"Binder said it's the client's decision, but the lawyer's job is to help clients think through their decisions. Often they think only short term with only one goal in mind. If you pave paradise, what will your friends and family think? Do you think people will want to do business with you? What are the long-term economic effects? In a year how will you feel about yourself?"

"He told us," Sean says, "that big time corporate lawyers spend half their time telling CEOs that what they want to do, while legal, is a bad idea. I was thrilled; I was on the moral outrage side. I was even upset that Binder sold the lyrics."

"OK," says Lucy, "I'll try. I'll ask her what her friends will think. Would her deceased husband approve? Does she want to be remembered as someone who rejected her son? Does she realize she's inflicting a lifetime of pain? It might work. I'll make sure her caregiver isn't there."

"Ask her what Jesus would do." Lucy can't tell if Sean is being sincere or snide.

"Let's start with the caregiver," Franks says, "Google her. Maybe she's up to no good. That would help. Let's see what the client wants to do after Lucy talks to her. If she insists, we can always withdraw. It's her money, and there's always the guy down the street."

Sean winks at Lucy. "How come it's always the 'guy' down the street and not the 'girl' down the street?"

"Woman," Lucy winks back.

CHAPTER TWENTY

Lucy's glad she has work to do.

Why doesn't he call? Maybe we're done.

Number one on her to-do list "Dirt on Roberta Roberts." Reading Roberta's Facebook page, Lucy discovers she is fifty-two, moves often, changes friends more than some men change their underwear, and is in and out of money. One month she is buying designer clothes and expensive bling that looks trashy to Lucy, the next month complaining her electricity might be turned off.

Roberta has an old DUI conviction, a few misdemeanor arrests for theft, all dropped, but then *bingo*. Dirt! In 2008 she was charged with theft for defrauding Iris Goodwin, an elderly woman in her care. She'd persuaded Iris to buy her a car, jewelry, and other expensive gifts. A conviction would be great but the charges were dismissed. That doesn't prove anything, maybe the victim died, had dementia, or the prosecutor had more pressing matters.

Not bad. Dirt, pay dirt. Lucy turns off her computer and scrolls through her email.

Damn, I should never have made a political donation. Now that's all I get. Why should I give money to a Dennis Johnson running for city council in McCallsburg, Iowa, even if my gift will be tripled?

Delete, delete, delete. Finally a message from Clay. "Want to get dinner Friday night?"

Her mood soars. Celebrate.

But wait. He didn't say, "Sorry," or "I miss you." Why should he be sorry? I screwed up. Maybe he wants to end it. But that's OK. We haven't dated that long. I won't be heartbroken. I'm too busy for a relationship. He isn't worth caring about.

She calls his cell.

"Clay."

"Hi, it's me, Lucy."

For a moment neither speaks. "Dinner sounds good. Where?"

Clay suggests a time and place and hangs up.

He didn't sound that friendly, but that doesn't mean anything. He's at work. Too busy to talk. Shit, I'll find out at dinner. Back to work. I should talk to Mary's son. Ask him about her mental capacity but don't tell him he's getting cut out of the will; that would be privileged. What should I wear for dinner?

She calls. Roberta answers.

"Mary's asleep. Can I help you?"

"No, you can't. I'm her lawyer and this is legal business. Wake her if you have to." Lucy is in no mood to put up with a lot of shit. Roberta puts her on hold. Seconds pass, minutes.

Usually patient, Lucy feels herself getting angry.

"Hi Lucy, this is Mary."

"Sorry to wake you but I need to talk with your son."

"I wasn't sleeping," Mary whispers. "Why talk to him? You won't persuade me to change my mind. We're a Christian family. Churchgoers. None of this queer business."

"I won't try to change your mind. I just want to make sure when we change the will it can't be thrown out—make it foolproof."

Lucy knows full well that she doesn't have to talk to the son to make the will foolproof. Shakespeare advised, "Do a great right by doing a little wrong." Perhaps she can bring the family together and her client won't die estranged from her son. A great good. Overstating legal uncertainty, a little wrong.

"OK, Lucy. Call my son," says Mary and, in a louder voice, "I want to make sure Roberta gets my money,"

Lucy calls. No answer. "Gerald, my name is Lucy Wagner; I'm your mom's lawyer. I need to ask you a couple questions. Please call me at 425-1589. Thanks." Had she said her number too fast? She hates it if she has to listen to the message a couple times to get the right number.

Five minutes later, "Hi, It's Gerald Smith, returning your call. Are you sure you have the right Gerald Smith? My mom is in hospice. What does she need a lawyer for?"

"I'm sorry about your mom's condition. But you're the right person. She hired me to update her will. Need to talk to you about that."

"Ummm. Call me Jerry. I don't know what to say. I know she and my dad wrote wills. I assumed they'd leave most of their money to a charity, Teens On their Own. Mom was a big supporter and a volunteer."

"Have you talked with her recently? How do you think she's doing?"

"We're not talking. We had a fight a couple of months ago, not sure what it was about."

Probably about him being "queer." Screw privilege.

"I don't know any delicate way to tell you this, but she told me she wants to cut you out because you're gay, although 'gay' wasn't the word she used."

Jerry laughs. "She never minced her words." He pauses, "I am."

What am I supposed to say? "Congratulations" seems inappropriate.

"She wants to leave all her money to Roberta Roberts, her caregiver."

"I met her a couple times. She seemed pushy and overprotective of Mom. You're sure mom wants to leave her all her money? I don't want the money, I'm doing fine, but if not me, at least to some charity. Dad always talked about that."

"It's fishy. Bequests to caregivers are suspect."

"Persuade her to give it to the AIDS Project," Jerry laughs. Lucy likes him.

"Seriously, this Roberta might be a con artist. She was charged with theft of an older person's money."

"This gay business isn't like my mom. She's very tolerant. When I was a kid, a black family moved into our neighborhood and, to put it mildly, some neighbors weren't happy. 'Black' wasn't the word they used. My mom invited them to dinner."

"People change when they get older. The world is changing so quickly. Cell phones, Google, and even gay marriage. They get scared and confused."

Should I have mentioned gay marriage? Tell him I'm fine with it. Better not, it'll probably come out as condescending.

"Everyone's confused. I've stopped watching the news. I wish I could talk with my mom. Love to hear her not mince words about the president. And there's something she needs to know. Alan, my partner, and I've been trying to adopt. We just got approved. She's going to be a grandmother."

Lucy likes him even better. The world is changing.

CHAPTER TWENTY-ONE

Not long ago many college graduates joined the military, now a mere trickle. Very few Americans know a soldier. Neither Frank nor Sean served. Their dads did, but neither talked much about it. Partly out of guilt, partly out of a desire to learn what his dad went through, but mostly because you can't say no to Manny, Sean volunteers a couple hours a week in Manny's Veteran Treatment Court.

"Manny Mejias, judge, United States Marines."

"Jody Williams, court clerk, Navy."

"Bob Boyd, veteran affairs, Army."

And so it goes, bailiff, legal intern, court reporter, standing at attention facing the thirty or so vets in the audience, a few fresh off the streets, others in Goodwill garb, two in suits.

"Tucson Veterans Treatment Court is now in session." Judge Mejias takes his seat. "Let's get started."

Sean is thankful to sit. He'll do a lot of standing this afternoon.

Behind the podium, United States and Arizona flags. On vet court day the flag of the Marine Corps is added. A gift from three law students, vets, who helped start the treatment court and pushed the law school into opening a clinic to help veterans.

"Mr. Ted Robins, please approach," calls the bailiff.

Ted slowly walks forward, dejected. Trouble yet again. Layers of ill-fitting clothing, uncomfortable in the Tucson heat, are clear indications he's homeless. He sees everyone stand. To honor him. This has never happened, he doesn't know whether to smile or run. He smiles.

Judy Evans, Coast Guard, a third-year law student, represents him. Sean sits at counsel table. Sean's there to advise Judy if she runs into trouble. She never does. He tries to look professional while sneaking looks at his iPhone for "breaking news" or movie reviews.

At the prosecutor's table a young woman reads files for tomorrow's court. Prosecutors don't have much to do because the judge decides who stays in the program and who gets kicked out. They're mostly a formality.

Even though he has to stand, Sean smiles.

It's great they call him "Mr. Robins." Probably on the street he's known as "Homeless guy," "Hey you," and "Bum." Worse when he's drunk.

He was arrested for public intoxication and public urination. He signed a citation promising to appear in court. He didn't. Fearful of jail, many vets don't. Warrants are issued, even traffic stops trigger arrests, and then it's likely jail. Sean's never feared a traffic stop or been in jail. He recalls a law prof saying everyone involved in criminal justice should spend a night in jail— police, judges, lawyers, but apparently not law professors.

"Has Ms. Evans explained your options?"

"Yes, Your Honor. Go to trial, plead guilty, or go in the VA program."

"How do you plead, Mr. Robins?"

"Judge Mejias, I'm guilty. I drink too much. I need help." *Mister* Robins stands tall, speaks loud. Dignity rocks. "I'm worried about Bandit, my dog. I can't take her to rehab. She's all I have. She protects me, loves me," Robins almost cries.

No one knows what to say. Finally Judy steps up, a fellow soldier needs her help. "I have a fenced backyard and love dogs. I'll take care of Bandit until you're on your feet."

Sean spends an afternoon at the VA to learn what is in store for the vets. He's surprised how large it is. Numerous buildings, parking lots full, lots of construction, people milling around, and two guys sitting on a bench talking.

"When they get here they're evaluated," says Beth, an intake worker. "There are programs for job training, domestic violence, substance abuse counseling, health care, and even help with housing. Free coffee and donuts."

Too bad I stopped at Dutch Bros on the way. They have terrific coffee, but free is free.

The crowded lobby isn't just young men. Some older, some younger, some men, some women, some haggard, some neat, some tatted, some bearded, some disabled, some hostile, but most friendly and eager to talk.

"I didn't join to kick down doors. I joined to serve, to rescue kids in floods."

"The army is one of the few places a black can get a break."

"Hypervigilance is great in deployment, not so good at Starbucks."

"Things are better now. I got spat on when I got back from Nam."

"A lot of guys hated the Army. I didn't love it but I learned I could do things I never thought I could."

"The worst days of my life and the best days of my life were in Afghanistan, often the same day."

"If it weren't for my leg, I'd go back, in a heartbeat."

"Happiest day in my life when I got out."

"I'm not a hero. I forecasted the weather in Afghanistan. Hot today, hotter tomorrow."

"I grew up in San Francisco and went to Harvard. No one gives a shit when you're outside the wire. My best buddy was an Okie who barely got out of high school."

"Thanks for your service gets you 10% off on Tuesdays."

A slight, soft spoken Hispanic woman who had lost a leg recalls: *"I was shot, on the ground, surrounded by soldiers. Bullets, smoke, screams everywhere. I thought I was going to die, never to see my parents again, making my peace with God. Yet I knew my buddies would die for me and I would die for them. I never felt so safe in my life."*

When Sean's back in his car and alone what the vets said swirls in his head. I've never felt that safe, that close to people. Law practice is dog-eat-dog. We're competitive, not fulfilling a mission. If I die it will be from stress or overindulging in food or alcohol. No one would die for me or vice versa. My life's been too predictable, too safe, too easy.

CHAPTER TWENTY-TWO

Friday afternoon. Sean, it's his turn, brings the pastries and, of course, a special treat for Dusty, a Sonoran hot dog minus the bun. They complain about the weather, discuss the new Japanese restaurant—Lucy heard it's great even if you don't like sushi—and what did Richard Bell, a renowned plaintiffs' lawyer do with the money. He was indicted for stealing tens of thousands of dollars from his clients.

"He's a pretty boring guy," says Sean. "Probably not a woman or lavish trips to Vegas, more likely up his nose or into his arm."

The topic turns to the Continuing Legal Education class Sean went to yesterday.

During the Civil Rights Movement lawyers stood tall, fighting injustice, making the world better, *Brown v. Board of Education*. They were heroes. Not so much during Watergate. Lawyers lied, covered up. Law schools rushed to require ethics courses and state bars required lawyers to take CLEs on ethics. Whether they make lawyers more ethical is questionable but they flag issues lawyers might face and get them thinking.

"It was on ethics, surprisingly interesting. About the obligation to keep client confidences."

Shit. Telling Jerry his mother planned to cut him out. Clear violation. But if I hadn't things wouldn't have worked out.

"What if your client tells you he plans to kill someone? Not that he *did* kill someone, that would be privileged, even where he buried the body." Sean pauses. "But future crimes aren't covered. So you *can* tell the cops. The question is *must* you tell the cops?"

"And?" asks Frank.

"There was an interesting case in California. A patient told his psychiatrist he was planning to kill someone. The psychiatrist didn't warn the victim. The widow sued on the theory he had a duty to warn and won big bucks."

"No right answer?" asks Frank.

"There is," says Sean. "Never ask a client if they plan to kill someone. Lucy, what's new on your hospice case?"

"Mary isn't rewriting her will. I talked with her son, Jerry. Good guy. He didn't care about the money, only wanted to make up with his mom."

Thankfully Frank doesn't spot the breach of confidence issue but he sees another. "You had Mary's permission to talk to her son?"

"Yeah, kind of pushed her," Lucy hurries on, "I had Jerry come with me to the hospice and wait outside while I talked to his mother. Her caregiver, Roberta, was there. She's always there. I told her she had to leave the room. She got huffy but when I asked 'Do you remember a woman name of Iris Goodwin?' she glared, slammed the door. Last anyone saw of her."

"OK, Florence Nightingale, tell us how you worked everything out and how everyone hugged, except Roberta." Sean, a tad cynical, adds, "Mary Poppins of the law."

Why does Sean do this? I need to stand up to him.

"Well, Mary Poppins did well," Lucy smiles. "Jerry and his partner are adopting. Mary cried when Jerry told her, decided not to change her will, and realized she has to hang on to hold the baby."

"Wonderful," says Frank. Sean smiles.

"There goes another fee."

"Come on, Sean. We didn't get into this business only to make money. And maybe Jerry will need a lawyer. Lucy, good lawyering, helping folks through difficult times."

"I'm an asshole," Sean says. "Don't mind me. Great lawyering. I hear you've brought in several cases."

Great lawyering. Bringing a family together. New cases. How can they not hire me?

"Yesterday I brought in a guardianship, the client's grandmother has lost it and can't handle her finances. She's bought hundreds of dollars of magazines she doesn't read, talks to people on the shopping network everyday, and has spent a fortune on clothes and jewelry she'll never wear. She contributes to anyone who comes to the door. She's almost depleted her savings."

"I'll be dropping by, what's her address?" asks Sean.

Lucy had always planned to do criminal defense, although most of what she knew came from novels and movies. Her career goals began to change after second year in law school. She had a summer clerking job at the Gibson firm. She worked on a contract case. Their client, the Stiggalls, had contracted with Desert Builders to build their dream house in the Tucson Mountains. They had drawn up very detailed plans and, in the contract, the builders promised to follow them. They didn't get it perfect. One of the walls on the patio was twelve inches off. Desert Builders had breached the contract. The legal question was how much should they pay to make things right?

The builders said it wasn't done on purpose and it would cost about $10,000 to move the wall. Four realtors signed an affidavit stating the location of the wall would make no difference in the worth of the house. The Stiggalls said they wanted the house they were promised. Should the Stiggalls get $10,000, replacement cost, or nothing?

Lucy first looked in the Arizona statutes, and found no answer. She had no better luck searching Arizona case law, no Arizona court had ruled on the issue. She then turned to how other states had ruled. The rulings would be persuasive to an Arizona court, but, alas, she found cases going both ways.

"It will be a case of first impression," Lucy told Gibson, the senior partner.

"What's their best argument that the wall shouldn't be replaced?"

"Economic waste. It caused no real harm. If you're negligent and brush up against someone but do no damage, they can't sue you and argue, 'You shouldn't have done that'. And if the Stiggalls get the $10,000, they might simply pocket it."

"Good. And ours?"

"If the court gives our clients nothing, that would encourage builders to be sloppy."

"Not bad. We'll be hiring some new associates next year. Apply."

Her drift away from criminal law continued when she tried two cases as a student in the law school's Criminal Defense Clinic. She won the simple assault case; the victim showed up drunk. The DUI was a sure loser, bad driving, high blood alcohol, a video showing unsteady walking, and the drunk's traditional rant, "Why aren't you out arresting real criminals?"

The experience was extremely valuable, but not in the expected way. She learned she doesn't like talking in front of a group of strangers, and doesn't like confrontation or arguing that Darth Vader isn't that bad a guy. As to criminal defendants, sure they have their rights, and she didn't mind the tattoos or the lies, but did mind those who would leer and ask, "Are you a full-service lawyer?"

Later Lucy learned it wasn't only criminal defendants who leer.

The irony is that her first job was with the public defender's office.

One never knows.

CHAPTER TWENTY-THREE

Lucy wakes up, confused.

A *bad dream? No. What? Work? Clay? No, fuck, Joyce's memorial service.*

Drinks coffee, feeds Teddy, and thinks about what to wear. She hasn't been to a funeral since her Uncle Stephan died so many years ago. She had worn pantyhose with her long-sleeved black dress that fell below her knees. Appropriate church attire. Since this isn't at a church or a cemetery and it's Tucson, she opts for her go-to black pants and red v-neck silk shirt. At the last minute, she switches to turquoise. Black and red are too festive.

The service is at a Polish hall on the East side of town. Lucy knows Joyce's grandparents are Polish, but she's never heard of a Polish hall. She gets directions on her phone; it's further away than she thought.

She hurries to her car. Tries to start it. Nothing happens.

Shit, shit, shit. Is the day going to get worse? How many Poles does it take to start a car? Not funny. This old Honda will give me trouble but, please, not today. Start! Shit, must be the battery. Too late to call AAA. Uber. I'll be late. I need a new car.

Lucy still has school loans and a huge Payday Loan. Against all her instincts—even druggies had advised against it—desperate for drugs she'd taken out a Payday Loan. She couldn't make a payment and took out another loan to pay it. Again and again. Always another. It's known as the "debt trap." Slowly, she'd been paying off everything.

New car?

Ha.

The Uber driver arrives. He's young, brown curly hair, kinda cute, and too inquisitive. "How long you lived in Tucson? . . . What's your favorite group? . . . You don't like music? Everyone likes music."

She finally says, "I'm going to a funeral and I don't feel like music or talking."

"I'm so sorry. I wish I would've known. I should of kept my trap shut, but I talk too much. Who died?"

"Please, I don't want to talk."

"OK, I get it. My girl's always telling me to shut the fuck up. Think there'll be music?"

Lucy feels like screaming. Finally they arrive. Not late. In the lobby a neatly dressed young man hands her a brochure with a picture of Joyce on the front and a short bio on the back.

Inside about thirty people sit on folding chairs. No one is dressed in black and red or wears pantyhose. There are a couple in turquoise. The room is stark and ice cold. Air conditioning was a great invention but buildings in Tucson are often too cold. An older man and woman, Joyce's parents, and maybe a brother, sit in the front row. Lucy recognizes Ellie, Karen, Suzi, Bobby-Jo, and a few women from Serenity House whose names she doesn't remember. She takes a seat next to Bobby-Jo.

An older, gray-haired man wearing a stylish suit walks to the podium. "Good afternoon, everyone. My name is Bernard Miller; friends call me Bernie. I'm not a clergyman, but Joyce's family has asked me to help celebrate Joyce's life."

In today's world funerals have become "celebrations of life." What's to celebrate when a young woman dies of a drug overdose?

"We'll begin with some music."

Two young men, one with a guitar and the other with another string instrument approach the podium. Lucy's not sure what the other instrument is. She'd never taken music lessons, been in a band or even a choir. "We're going to play two of Joyce's favorites, *Desperado* and *Bobby-McGee*."

Bernie then reads a poem or a psalm, Lucy isn't sure. She's not a church person but it's moving He begins talking about Joyce. "She was always friendly and someone you could count on . . ."

Friendly and someone to count on? Not the Joyce I knew. Does Bernie know she was a drug addict? They're not friendly, they lie, they don't keep their promises—mostly the promises they make to themselves. At my funeral I want someone who knows me to talk, mistakes and all.

Bernie asks if anyone in the audience wants to speak. Ellie raises her hand. "I'm Ellie Rosenblatt, the director of Serenity House. Joyce left us prematurely. Another victim of the opioid epidemic."

Ellie is smart, articulate, and compassionate. Her resume screams CEO yet she looks more like the grandma in a 1950s novel.

"When I remember Joyce I want to remember a girl with success, a girl who completed rehab at Serenity House and graduated from drug court. Joyce had ten months clean before she died. Those in the program know that's a tremendous accomplishment. Many never complete the program, never stay clean for more than a few days. To an addict, ten days without drugs seem like ten years."

Lucy looks at Joyce's parents and wonders what they are thinking.

"Joyce had a productive life before and after drugs. She'd almost completed college and was trying to finish up these last months. She had a job. She reconciled with her parents, who are here today. She got her health back."

Lucy hears sobbing but is distracted by thoughts of her own recovery.

"Each of us needs to remember it's OK to ask for help. Relapse is part of recovery. Call us. Call your sponsor or mentor, or even a friend."

Is she talking to me?

Others speak about Joyce. Some about special moments with her. A woman named Brandy says, "I was going to leave Serenity House. I knew I couldn't make it. Joyce spent a couple hours with me and shared how she had felt like that before, that the moment would pass. Because of her I'm in outpatient and doing well."

Another woman talks on and on about her own struggles. She

barely mentions Joyce.

Can you 86 people from your funeral? I mean, your celebration of life.

Two childhood friends talk about the fun stuff they did and the trouble they avoided. A wonderful change of pace. People laugh, including Joyce's parents.

Bernie, who didn't know Joyce very well, knows his celebrations of life. He takes the mike. "Thank you for those wonderful stories. I'm sure everyone in the room wishes they knew Joyce better. Anyone else want to share?"

I should. I can't. I want to tell people how hard recovery is. Tell her family how strong Joyce was. But I can't get up there. I couldn't hold it together, but maybe that would be OK. Once it's over, I'll never have the chance.

No one else raises their hand. "OK. We'll end this with a few more of Joyce's favorite songs," says Bernie. "The family has provided lunch and hopes everyone will stay."

Shit, I should have said something. I owed it to Joyce, to everyone here, but mostly to me.

"Lucy, let's go get some grub," says the ever practical Bobby-Jo. "Heard it's a good spread. Joyce's parents have money." Life goes on. Lucy follows Bobby-Jo. She wants to leave but she knows it's a bad idea to be home alone today. She's sad, worried, and vulnerable.

She smells tomato sauce and Italian spices. The table is lavish. Salads, dishes of lasagna, each a tad different, chicken parmesan, lemon cake, tiramisu, and chocolate something. Not typical Polish cuisine. No pierogis.

Bobby-Jo heaps enough on her plate for two large laborers who haven't eaten in days. Lucy takes a lot of salad, a small amount of pasta, and a piece of lemon cake. There will be plenty left if she's still hungry.

They're joined by Suzi and a woman Lucy doesn't know. "I'm Anne, a new counselor at Serenity House."

"I'm Lucy, I'm a graduate."

"She's a lawyer," says Bobby-Jo.

"That's great. My daughter's only in high school, but that's what she wants to do," says Anne.

"Don't let anyone talk her out of it. Lots of school, but it's worth it."

After a few minutes of talk about the service and the food, Anne says, "Maybe Joyce took her own life. I saw her a few days before she died. She seemed to be doing well, running groups. A relapse leads to depression, loss of self-worth. Joyce may have felt she let everyone down. Suicide is six times more likely for addicts. I'm not saying she did, but it's possible."

Anne said she was new. She couldn't have known Joyce well. Another rush to judgment.

"Maybe she didn't kill herself," says Suzi. "Maybe she couldn't tolerate the dose and it was an accident. Or maybe it was laced with Fentanyl. They sell it that way nowadays."

Harold? I'll get him somehow.

Talk returns to the ceremony, Bernie, and the food. There's even a Polish joke. But small talk doesn't keep fear at bay. They're addicts. Suicide or overdose, one of their number is dead.

One wonderful hit never hurt anyone.

CHAPTER TWENTY-FOUR

Lucy's nervous.

"Lucy, let's grab lunch. It's on the firm."

Is this it? "We're sorry but. . . ?"

Frank's in a good mood but when he insists on taking a corner table, out of earshot, things look bad. But there's hope. He smiles.

"Lucy, Sean and I are very pleased with your work. Getting the hospice client back with her son was brilliant. You show a great deal of creativity in your research. We're glad because that means Sean and I don't have to do any. You'll be a terrific lawyer."

Maybe it won't be a "sorry but" after all. Maybe it's a permanent offer? What the hell, it's on the firm.

"I'll have the special salad, with chicken."

Frank orders a burger and pauses a few minutes, looks hard at Lucy.

"But."

Shit.

"The problem is your addiction. A classmate of mine was disbarred because she was high while trying a case. Did a terrible job, a guy convicted when he shouldn't have been. The good news is that when the appellate court found out, they reversed. He'd already done two years. But who knows how many others she'd hurt."

Will I always be a marked woman?

Not raising her voice, "I've been clean for two years."

"So was she. I'm not being judgmental. In high school I was into drugs. I even sold. But a couple of my homies killed a guy, drug deal gone bad. I wasn't involved and never got arrested, but I knew if I didn't do something I'd be in prison or dead."

Frank selling drugs. Does Marie know?

"How did you get out?"

"Wasn't easy. A priest, Father Fintan. He took me and a couple of others under his wing. We would meet once or twice a week and talk about drugs, violence, and how we could be men without gold chains, without low riders, and without mad dog stares. Not too much Jesus but He was always in the background."

"How did you get away from your friends?"

"The hard part, realizing they weren't my friends. Then it was easy. When they asked me to party I'd say, "I have better things to do." And I did. Father Fintan kept us so busy we didn't have time to hang out. Cleaning the yards of old folks who couldn't."

Frank falls silent, thinking back to those happy days, of those friends, and of Father Fintan. He smiles, "Even the yards of nonbelievers. They always gave us cookies and some cried. Those folks and Father Fintan are why I became a lawyer."

Shit. I became a lawyer because I liked crime novels.

She forces a laugh. "Most recovery programs don't put people to work. How long have you been clean?"

"Close to twenty years. But I haven't recovered; I'm still in recovery. Drugs are always there. If things go badly, who knows?"

Being understanding takes you only so far. Now serious, Frank suddenly asks, "If I tell you you're fired, would you go home and get high?"

Lucy feels like she's been hit.

Yeah maybe. Probably. If things go bad I'm tempted. I've gotta seem positive.

"No. I've overcome a lot," she mumbles.

"Don't worry. I'm not firing you, but we're not sure if we can make you an offer. Eat your salad."

"Is this going to follow me always? I never decided to get into drugs."

"Now you're being judgmental. The question isn't how you got in but if you're staying out."

They fall silent and no, they don't want dessert, but refills would be nice.

"You hired me knowing of my past."

"I'm a believer in second chances, I got mine. But it's not only Sean and me taking a chance, so are our clients. You're doing fine but if you slip and screw up a client's case . . ."

That's not fair. I'm doing good. I won't screw up. Mary cried when she first held her new granddaughter. I did that. It's more than crime novels.

"I love being a lawyer. I want to help people. I've learned so much working for you guys. What can I do?"

"Stay sober, keep up the good work. If you ever feel too much pressure, tell me. I'm not a bad guy. And I'll never fire you for being honest. Have your sponsor call me if she thinks you are getting in trouble. We can go from there. We're on your side, but we can't put clients at risk."

There's hope.

"I still have a chance?"

The friendly Frank says, "Yes," but the unfriendly Frank adds, "But no third chance."

CHAPTER TWENTY-FIVE

Lucy suggests she and Clay meet at the restaurant. She wants to be able to leave if things don't go well. She doesn't want him driving her home if it's over. But why would he suggest dinner if he doesn't want to see her? He could dump her by email or text like everyone else does.

That afternoon Bobby-Jo calls several times. Leaves messages. Variations of, "I'm worried about your date with Clay. You can stay at my house tonight if you want. Promise me you'll call. You have hard-won sobriety and a lot to lose."

On the way to the restaurant Lucy can't keep her mind off Joyce's death. Her life had seemed to be going in a positive direction. She had a job, was finishing school, and had reconnected with her parents. She'd seemed so confident at the fundraiser. A date with the wrong guy? A bad day at work or school? Stumbled on a pill or the residual from a baggie of heroin and couldn't resist? Or maybe her old dealer made her an offer she couldn't refuse.

One wonderful hit never hurt anyone.

The medical examiner had found heroin and small amounts of fentanyl in Joyce's system. There was no evidence to prove she OD'd on purpose or with someone's help. He ruled it accidental. A kindness to the family?

Could Harold have anything to do with this? If he did, I'll—I'll what? And I helped Sean get him off. That asshole belongs in prison or worse.

Clay had suggested an Ethiopian restaurant south of downtown. Lucy's late, having tried on at least six different outfits. One had a stain, one was too fancy, one too casual. She settles for skinny jeans, a purple V-neck shirt, and sandals. Her mirror says she looks good.

She can't find a parking place. There are empty spaces, but signs that read *Permit Parking Only*. She parks in a dirt lot about three blocks away. The car runs fine now that she bought a new battery. Hopefully nothing else will need to be fixed. Batteries are expensive, but worse, she doesn't want to ride with a motormouth Uber driver.

Lucy doesn't mind the walk except it's a shady area of town littered with syringes, used condoms, and there's a faint smell of vomit. Men doing drug deals. Temptation. She walks fast, not making eye contact with the men she passes.

"Hey babe, nice ass," one of them calls.

Men. I wish I knew something to say to that jerk so he would feel dirty when he talks about my body. Good or bad. What makes guys think they can comment publicly about my ass or any other part of me? If I said, "nice ass'" to a strange guy I might get raped. Guys can wear whatever they want and no one cares. If my dress is too short or my shirt too low and a guy tries to rape me, it's my fault. If I kiss a guy and then say no, then I'm a tease.

She finally reaches the restaurant. She spies Clay immediately as there are only six or seven small tables.

"Hi, Clay." He's at a table, not a booth.

Is that deliberate? They can't sit close. Don't be stupid and overthink everything.

"Sorry I'm late."

"Only a few minutes."

"I had trouble finding parking."

"It's not the greatest neighborhood. I'll drive you back to your car." A good sign. "Have you eaten here before?"

"No, I've never had Ethiopian food." The only thing she remembers about Ethiopia is that around the l980s or 90s a hundred thousand Ethiopian Jews were resettled in Israel. Her college boyfriend was a zealous Zionist. He loved to lecture people about the importance of Israel. Always took Israel's side. She pretended to agree, but wasn't sure what to think. Maybe their relationship had ended because she isn't Jewish or because she doesn't always support Israel or maybe because he was an opinionated jerk.

The waiter drops off a menu and takes their drink order. Clay orders a mint tea and she does too. There's a list of Ethiopian beers but why take a chance.

"The food here is terrific and cheap. I usually order the meat combination plate. You can pick from several choices, chicken or beef with different sauces and vegetables. They have a veggie combo too." Ignoring the warnings of the A.M.A, Lucy orders the beef combination. She has reached her weight loss goal and more. The last few pounds slid off. She hadn't felt much like eating since her relationship with Clay had gone south.

One of the things she likes about Clay is how easy he is to be with. Tonight's different. There's tension. If only she could go back in time and never have looked at his phone.

"How's your job?" Clay breaks the awkward silence.

"Going well. I like doing a bunch of different things, not just writing motions. We have office meetings and discuss cases. I'm learning a lot. Cindy, our legal secretary, is smart and gorgeous. We've become friends. You'll have to meet her. And we have a great office dog."

I'm rambling. I hope he doesn't meet Cindy. I better shut up and let him say something. Tell him about my feelings about criminal law? I don't want to spend my life helping the likes of Harold Olsen or even Jordan.

"I kind of decided I'm not cut out to be a criminal defense lawyer. It's too confrontational."

Lucy hears a dog barking and turns to look out the window. A man is walking a brindle colored pit-bull that pulls on his leash trying to go after a large mixed-breed brown dog being walked across the street. Both watch until the dogs are out of sight.

"I hear ya. I didn't like being a trial lawyer. The prosecutors don't care about justice, just winning. And the judges think they're really hot shit. Black robe disease."

It's great to have a neutral topic. To keep it going Lucy asks, "Why do you stay at the PD?" but realizes too late it sounds like she's interviewing him for a job.

"I like my colleagues. I like reading cases and figuring out new arguments."

The waiter brings their food. Lucy smells cinnamon, cardamon, and ginger — some of her favorite spices. She can't wait to dig in. She hasn't eaten a decent meal since she and Clay fought.

Both start to eat as soon as the plates hit the table. No need to talk. Lucy realizes she's scarfed down almost half her food in a couple minutes. Another silence. "Did you finish telling me why you stayed at the PD?" An interview is better than silence.

The food is delicious but the mint tea taste likes sewer water. A beer'd be nice, but she doesn't want to drink if she has to drive.

"I like appellate work. Trial lawyers give me a ton of shit about sitting in my office leisurely reading transcripts and cases. But if they need help with the law, they ask me. We might not try jury trials, but the trial lawyers don't have to argue death cases in front of the Arizona Supreme Court. I had to argue tying someone up, putting them in a sack, and throwing them in a lake is not heinous behavior and doesn't justify the death penalty."

Splash.

"I've found my niche in elder law. Wills, estate planning, guardianships. I like helping people."

"Good for you. I'm sure you'll do a great job."

"Anything else?" the waiter asks.

"No," both reply.

"One check?"

"Yes," says Clay.

"Two," says Lucy at the same time. They both laugh. Clay smiles at her. The tension ebbs. It's now or never.

"I'm really, really sorry I looked at your phone. It was immature and there was no reason for it. I want to try to explain."

Clay says nothing, his smile gone.

She doesn't want to tell him she had been, was, is a drug addict.

What the hell. If I don't tell him we're probably done. If Phelps and Stone can tell the world about their mental illness, I should be able to tell my boyfriend. I hope he's going to stay my boyfriend.

"I was in a serious auto accident in law school. Driving home from dinner I had the right of way when this small white truck ran a red light. We were going to crash. I braked. The last thing I remember was the other driver's terrified eyes. I woke up in the hospital in a lot of pain with a concussion, broken ribs, lots of bruises. The doc gave me a prescription for oxycodone."

Lucy stops, tries not to cry. "I used more pills than I should have. Kept telling myself I'd stop, after finals. I couldn't study or focus because of the pain. I needed something to get me through."

"You don't have to tell me this, Lucy."

"Yes, I do. I kept getting prescriptions from my orthopedic doc till he cut me off. Then I found sleazy doctors who sell you as many pills as you want as long as you can pay. They charge a lot. When I ran out of pills, I went into withdrawal, which was way worse than I imagined. I was shaky, and anxious. I had a fever and threw up. I'd be sweaty and hot one minute and freezing the next. I couldn't stand still. I couldn't sleep. I started using heroin. It's cheaper. I never shot it, just smoked. My stupid rationalization. Never shot it. Addicts lie to themselves."

Lucy begins to cry.

"Lucy, I'm sorry. Do you want another tea or some water."

"No, let me finish. I finally realized I had a problem and went to rehab. It wasn't easy, but I kicked it. I've been clean two years. That's why it took me so long to get into the bar."

For a time Clay is quiet. "I don't know what to say. I started smoking when I was fifteen, tried to quit several times. Couldn't. When I got accepted at law school I promised myself I'd quit, but I didn't. Only made it two weeks. Then I promised myself after first year finals, but I didn't. When second year started, I tried again using nicotine gum, but that didn't work. I finally quit after I took the bar. Just stopped. For two weeks I was a wreck physically and mentally. Quitting was the hardest thing I've ever done. I'm sure what you went through was worse."

"Giving up any addiction is hard. Some say smoking is harder than heroin."

Bullshit.

"I like you, Lucy. Everything was going great, I thought. I was really angry you didn't trust me."

"I had some bad experiences with men. They lied to me, cheated on me, stole from me. One hit me. I probably picked losers. It's hard to believe that someone smart and kind and normal would like me. That's why I checked up. I doubt I'm explaining it right."

Clay laughs, "Normal, me? I want to keep seeing you, but you have to promise you'll try to trust me."

"I promise."

"If you have a concern about me talk to me. I won't lie to you."

"I promise. I feel so stupid I got jealous of your hairdresser."

"But you know she's pretty hot."

He smiles and they both laugh.

Lucy's relieved knowing he still likes her. Maybe her life will work out.

Maybe I shouldn't have driven my car.

CHAPTER TWENTY-SIX

"Staying late again?" Sean peeks into Frank's office. Frank doesn't look happy. Piles of files, coffee cups.

"Don't you remember Jordan's trial starts tomorrow, you jerk. I'll be up half the night rereading the file. Every time I do something new jumps out."

"Yeah, I reread the files after each day in trial. Sometimes a witness says something that puts a new take on things. I'm going out to have a beer. I'll have one for you."

"Fucking prosecutors never should have charged this as a felony. Jordan would have pled to simple assault and everyone could get on with their lives. But no. Abby will have to testify and relive what happened."

"Is it a 'reasonable doubt' case or a 'my guy is innocent' case?" asks Sean.

"Not sure, we'll see how strong the prosecution case is. They'll call Abby, who will say she didn't consent, a friend who will say she heard Abby saying 'no,' a doctor who will say there was intercourse, and the police detective who will say Jordan lied. I've got something on all of them, but unless it goes brilliantly I don't think a 'reasonable doubt' argument will fly. I'll probably have to call Jordan and hope he can convince the jury he's innocent. But he might make things worse. Most defendants do. Sandra Knowles is prosecuting and does a mean cross."

"How are you going to handle Abby?"

"Two choices. Either I get her to admit with all the noise and foreplay Jordan could think she consented. If she insists he could have heard, I'll have to attack her suggesting that she consented but has changed her mind because she doesn't want to admit it."

"What about Jordan's lie?"

Frank frowns, shrugs. "Good night, Sean. Have one—make that two—for me."

Where to begin? Police reports, medical reports, witness statements? This kid doesn't belong in prison. Shouldn't have to register for life as a sex offender. It's on me, I can't fuck up.

After an hour of broken pencils, curses, and insights, McDonalds. Despite worries about his weight, it's "two Big Macs and large fries, pay at the second window." He plans to give half of one to Dusty. The bigger half. Unfortunately for Dusty it doesn't work out. He's snoring. It would be cruel to wake him. Frank calls home.

"Hi, Marie, won't be home till late." Frank looks at the file and it seems like he hasn't made a dent. "Real late."

In his second year of law school he met Marie, an undergraduate studying to become a teacher. "Hi, I'm a law student" was the traditional pick up line at Starbucks. Marie wasn't impressed but was taken with Frank's T-shirt, a picture of a Golden Retriever with "Whoever said diamonds are a girl's best friend never had a dog" written below.

Marie teaches high school English and a class in Mexican Literature. A few years ago some state legislators called for the Mexican Lit class to be abolished. Teaching it undermines American Literature and will lead to revolution. Of course they have no idea what students read in American Lit.

Cooler heads prevailed, but maybe not forever. It's Arizona.

Even though Marie learned the Golden Retriever shirt belonged to Frank's roommate, they married a year after they met. Their parents were delighted. They'd been holding their breath, worried that their educated, integrated children would marry Anglos. They didn't. Something to brag about.

They're a happy couple. Two children and a dog, Sparkie. They have one ongoing argument. Marie wants to move to a bigger house, in a better neighborhood, with better schools, and fewer drugs. Frank wants to stay in the neighborhood he grew up in.

Successful Mexicans shouldn't move out they should stay and be role models.

"Don't stay too late," Marie says. "You need to get your sleep."

"No lawyer has gone to sleep during a trial or, for that matter, slept well the night before."

"Reheat the stew." Frank now regrets the second Big Mac.

"How was your class?" Frank makes small talk while he thinks about how to handle Jordan's lie.

"The students loved *Aunt Julia and the Script Writer.*"

Frank, getting back to the moment. "That's the guy who wrote several soaps and got all the characters mixed up. The actors praying their character isn't getting sick or moving to Poland. I loved it, almost finished it."

Frank has a bad, or maybe good, habit of not finishing books.

"Next week, Harry Potter."

"Good book, but no Mexicans. Maybe they should have a beaner bussed to Hogwarts."

"Not bussed, they take the train. Goodnight, Frank. Reheat the stew. See you in the morning."

Meanwhile, at Mr. Heads, Sean is on his second Pabst Blue Ribbon. He missed Happy Hour. Baseball blares on widescreen TVs. He has no interest in baseball, but what about his unexamined life?

Recently Lucy had returned from a funeral and asked him what he would want people to say at his eulogy. A stupid middle school assignment but, sitting alone, drinking a beer, why not? What would they say?

Sean graduated law school, was on Law Review. He
practiced law. Divorced. No children. He had a
wonderful dog and a good sense of humor. Thank you.

Surely there *has* to be more. Sean signals the bartender. "Another PBR. Any way to turn down the TV?"

"Sorry, the biker over there is a Cubs fan, even when they lose."

Tattoos, muscles, not a happy camper. Best to live with the sounds of baseball.

My mom never had a prestige job, never made money, but

there'd be a lot to say about her. Spent her life teaching and loving kids who would never graduate college, probably not even high school, kids who were avoided, kids she believed in.

And what about Frank? Married with two kids and a wife who taught high school. He coached soccer, as part of Rotary went to South America to install sanitation, toilets? Frank taught law school, taught writing to prisoners, and worked with the Minority Bar to help at-risk kids.

Pretty amazing guy. I'm lucky to be in practice with him.

Sean, never one to stay long in a funk, glances at the TV, the Cubs are down by five. Smiles.

And Sean never liked baseball.

CHAPTER TWENTY-SEVEN

Jordan wears a blue sports coat, red and blue striped tie, khaki pants, dress shoes. Nothing fancy, but respectful. Jury selection goes well. Judge Bennett doesn't let the prosecutors run the show. Eight jurors: five women and three men. You only get twelve if they want to kill you. Sandra Knowles, a prosecution star, keeps her opening brief, saving the inflammatory details for the witnesses and not promising too much. Promise Waldo, fail to produce Waldo, it's "Where's Waldo?"

Frank's opening is traditional. He talks a little about what a fine young man Jordan is, how this country is great because of the presumption of innocence and, looking directly at jurors, "Your duty, your sworn duty, is not to make up your minds until you hear both sides." Blah, blah blah.

The state's first witness, Kay Stone, is a volunteer at the Women's Crisis Center. Being a witness is no walk in the park. Even taking the oath is daunting, "Do you swear or affirm that you will tell the truth and nothing but the truth under penalty of perjury?" *Perjury?* There are flags and a high bench. The judge, in a black robe, stares down at you; lawyers shuffle files, ready to pounce, a somber and curious audience waits, hoping for a train wreck. All is quiet. You are it. All eyes on you.

Sandra: Ms. Stone, good morning. Please state your name and occupation for the record.

Kay gets through her direct testimony fairly well. Her primary responsibility is to counsel rape victims. She was on duty when Abby, crying and confused, came in. She calmed her down, held her hand, and assured her she'd be there for her. She told her what to expect, that it was good she hadn't showered as she'd have to have a physical examination to gather evidence.

Frank walks to the podium, introduces himself, smiles, and congratulates Kay for doing important work. In an oh-by-the-way tone, Frank gets her to agree that Abby wasn't eager to file a rape charge. He understands it is common, as victims tend to blame themselves. Feeling on safe ground, Kay explains that rape is seldom reported and men get away with it.

Kay: I told Abby it wasn't her fault. No matter what happened before, if you say, "no" and he doesn't stop, it's rape.

Frank had been hoping for this.

Frank: So your job was to convince Abby she had been raped.

No matter the answer, he's planted a doubt, hopefully a reasonable one. Sandra gives him a cold stare as he walks back to the defense table.

The state's next witness, Dr. Reed, one of the docs on call at the Women's Crisis Center, testifies that Abby was upset, that the exam is a humiliating ordeal for women, and there is no doubt she had sexual intercourse. He can't say if it was rape or consensual. Frank walks to the podium, all business.

Frank: Doctor Reed, were there bruises on her arms or shoulders?

Reed: Not that I could see.

Frank: But you looked?

Reed: Of course.

Frank: So no one held her down, hit her. Were there bruises around the vaginal area?

Reed: No.

Trial Practice 101: Quit when you're ahead. Never ask the dreaded "one question too many." But in the rush and adrenaline of trial, tired of bunts and singles, the left field bleachers loom. One swing. One question. Game over.

Frank: Now in your long experience isn't it a fact that if a woman was raped there would be bruises?

A question too many? You never know until you hear the answer.

Reed: No, that's not a fact. Often there aren't bruises. Abby could have easily been raped.

Trial Practice 101 cautions—the jury watches. Never show injury. Frank nods, thanks the doctor, and strolls confidently back to his chair. He convinces no one. Sandra smiles.

The first day doesn't go well. Back in his office Frank slams his file on the library table. Compassionate Sean greets the wounded warrior, "Maybe you should have taken Trial Practice 101."

"Calm down, Frank, it wasn't that bad. It's just the first day," Lucy says.

Frank ignores Sean. "Maybe Sandra won't call Crystal. She won't be a strong witness, maybe even help us, the ex-girlfriend who pressures Abby to call it rape. Lucy, how hard is it to persuade the jury that a woman scorned could lead her friend into lying?"

Shit, men believe all women think alike. That scorned women go berserk. That they manipulate their friends to do bad things? Well, come to think of it, in high school Nancy and her in-crowd pretty much destroyed Jimmy.

"It's possible."

"It's clear she's out to get Jordan, that business of her hearing Abby shouting," says Frank. "She didn't go in to save her or yell for help. Selling the idea that she pressured Abby will be harder."

"Sandy knows you'll be going after her," Sean says, "On direct she'll ask Crystal about her breakup with Jordan, about her saying she would get even. Crystal will get emotional and say she didn't mean it and that she would never pressure Abby to make a false accusation. Preemptive strike."

Lucy's confidence crashes. All she learned in Trial Practice 101 was how to impeach a witness with a prior inconsistent statement. "You now claim the light was red but didn't you tell your wife it was green?"

Lucy, wanting to remind folks she's there, says, "You should get in that Jordan will be kicked out of school. Have to register as a sex offender. Can't live where he wants. Create some sympathy."

"Good idea but I can't—not relevant, not admissible. The question's whether he knew she wasn't consenting. What happens to him in the future doesn't matter. Juries decide facts. Judges impose sentences."

"Well, yes," Lucy quickly covers her mistake, "but that's unfair. The jury will know Abby has been badly hurt and it will seem Jordan simply walks away."

Frank nods. "I think it was Dickens who said, 'the law's an ass.' "

"Bleak House," says Lucy recovering the high ground. "Someone said the law presumes a woman does what her husband tells her and the response was 'if the law presumes that, the law is an ass.' "

"Right on," says Sean.

CHAPTER TWENTY-EIGHT

Next morning, oatmeal. Frank's too nervous for anything heavy but the smell of bacon is too much. With a wink and a smile he takes a piece off Frank Junior's plate. Junior, still sleepy, isn't upset. He follows dad's lead and takes one off mom's plate. She frowns, "He's your son all right."

Breakfasts are Frank's favorite time—Marie, the kids, Sparkie. All together, planning the day, reviewing the week, laughing and joking, being a family. But today Frank's only half there. Should he put Jordan on the stand?

He drives his kids to school, the same school he went to.

Marie is wrong. Kennedy Elementary is a fine school. Did right by me. Mrs. Benson. What would she think about me being a lawyer? I don't know if Jordan can stand up to cross.

Frank wears a different tie. Not a different suit, a different tie. Down home guys, regular guys, don't have many suits. Corporate lawyers wear different suits everyday, handmade suits. They don't need to. They sit in their offices, review contracts, argue over the phone, worry about making partner. They only get out of the office for three-martini lunches. Deductible lunches, they trash clients over their third.

The courtroom is about a third full, mostly college kids. While they await the judge, Frank and Sandra exchange pleasantries with forced smiles. It is often said opposing lawyers, deep down, like each other. They don't.

"How's your boss's campaign going?"

"She'll be reelected. No one will vote for a criminal defense lawyer to be district attorney."

"Worse things could happen. Who are you calling first?"

"Crystal. Will you be calling Jordan?"

"Absolutely." Of course he isn't sure, but it's good to distract your opponent with false moves.

"I can't wait to cross All American boy." Bluffs work too.

Sandra's paralegal didn't do a great job telling Crystal how to dress. Yellow dress too short, too low cut, and too tight. Looks like she went for sexy in a dress borrowed from a thinner friend or from her, sigh, thinner self. She has enough gold bling for the starting five of an NBA basketball team.

Sandra opens with a few preliminary questions, Crystal's currently a student, was at the party, and knows Abby and Jordan. Then she moves in for the kill.

Sandra: What happened when you left the kitchen?

Crystal: I walked by the bedroom door, heard Abby crying "no." I didn't know what to do. Then Abby came out, crying, her clothes a mess.

Key testimony. But Sandra knows she has a problem. Sean was right, she draws the sting by bringing it up herself.

Sandra: Crystal, did you used to go out with Jordan?

Crystal: Yes, for a while and then he broke up with me.

Sandra: After you broke up what did you tell friends?

Crystal: I told them I would get even with him.

Sandra: But you wouldn't lie to this jury to get even with Jordan, would you?

Frank: Objection leading.

Judge Bennett: Sustained.

Sandra: Thank you, your honor. I'll rephrase the question. Crystal, would you lie to get even?

Crystal: I would never lie.

Sandra gives Frank a quick smile. He shouldn't have objected. Sandra's question was leading, telling Crystal to agree she wouldn't lie. However, in light of the objection, Sandra rephrased the question and Crystal gave a stronger answer, "I would never lie." But trial lawyers have only two or three seconds to make crucial decisions.

They make mistakes.

Frank, unfriendly and accusing, approaches the podium.

Frank: Crystal, you told friends you were out to get Jordan.

Crystal: I didn't mean it.

Lawyers need to listen. Not be wedded to their script. A witness trying to cover her tracks opens up new lines of attack.

Frank: You didn't mean it? You say things you don't mean?

Crystal: Maybe, sometimes.

Frank: When you told this jury that you heard Abby crying out, did you mean it?

Crystal doesn't answer. Frank moves on.

Frank: Wasn't there loud music at the party and drinking?

Crystal: I wasn't drunk and I heard her.

Frank: I didn't ask you if you were drunk or if you heard her. I asked about the music. Was there loud music?

Crystal: I guess.

Frank can't do better. When a witness ducks a question she comes across as someone who has a dog in the fight, as someone who might lie to protect her side, if not lie, at least spin the facts. Frank moves in for the kill.

Frank: Crystal, Abby is a good friend of yours. Yet you're telling this jury that for some reason you went and stood next to a bedroom door, heard Abby cry out, knew she was being raped, and you just stood there, doing nothing.

Frank pauses, shakes his head in disbelief.

Frank: *One final question, Crystal. Do you think your good friend Abby would tell you if she had consented, that Jordan didn't force her, and it wasn't rape?*

Sandra: Objection speculation.

Judge: *Sustained. Move on.*

Frank: Nothing further, Your Honor.

Sandra realizes calling Crystal was a mistake. She's a distraction. She doesn't want the jury arguing about Crystal. Abby will make or break this case.

CHAPTER TWENTY-NINE

Abby wears a conservative yet tasteful dress. Abby is cute, with short brown hair. She's about five foot six and 120 pounds compared to Jordan's six foot one and 190 pounds.

Her direct testimony begins as expected. She's a junior at the U, hopes to be a nurse, Jordan asked her to the party, they had been flirting, they danced and then went into the bedroom to talk and "maybe fool around."

Sandra: Then what happened?

Abby: Jordan got aggressive, told me he loved me, and got on top of me, held me down and . . . he raped me. I told him to stop more than once. I know he heard me, but he kept saying he knew I wanted it and kept going. It was horrible.

Several jurors shake their heads, a few stare at Jordan. Frank looks unconcerned. Jordan, as he was told, looks down, showing no reaction.

Sandra: You didn't consent?

Abby: I would never consent. I promised my parents and myself to remain a virgin. My big sister got pregnant and it tore my family apart.

Sandra's time to let things sink in. Abby, who has been looking at Sandra, suddenly turns to face Jordan.

Abby: Jordan, I liked you. I'll never trust a man again.

Trial Practice 101. End strong. Sandra took the class. Frank could object, there wasn't a question, but that would make things worse.

Sandra: Thank you. Nothing further.

Sandra rehearsed that, the bitch, Frank thinks as he walks to the podium. He is no longer unfriendly, accusing, but now a sympathetic father, a father correcting a mistaken child.

Frank: My name is Frank Perez and I represent Jordan. We know how stressful this must be for you. I won't be long, just a few questions. Is it OK to call you Abby?

Abby: Yes.

Frank: Now Abby, just to get things straight, no one forced you to go to the party.

Abby: No.

Frank: I know they are the rage, but no one forced you to wear a short dress.

Abby: No.

Frank: No one forced you to drink beer.

Abby: No.

Frank: Do you remember how many?

Abby: Not sure but not many.

Frank: It's hard to remember things after drinking, isn't it?

Abby: I wasn't drunk.

Frank: I didn't ask you if you were drunk. Did anyone force you into the bedroom?

Abby: No.

Frank: The music was so loud you couldn't even hear what was being said, isn't that right?

Abby: Yes. We wanted to talk.

Frank: Jordan didn't pull you in, push you in. You went of your own free will, isn't that right?

Abby: I didn't know what was going to happen.

Frank: Nothing did happen until you got on the bed with him and decided, in your words, to fool around.

Abby: I guess.

Frank: When you first arrived at the crisis center you were reluctant to call it rape. Why was that?

Abby: I thought maybe I had something to do with it.

Frank: And they convinced you it wasn't your fault, no matter what you did, that you were raped, isn't that a fact?

Abby: I don't remember exactly what they said but I was raped.

Frank: You promised yourself and your parents you would remain a virgin. Wouldn't it be hard for you to admit that you made a mistake and easier to convince yourself that you never consented?

Frank has made his point. He walks back to counsel table.

Judge Bennett: Abby, you're excused. You can remain in the courtroom if you wish.

Abby walks slowly to the gallery where she takes a seat next to her parents. She keeps her head down and doesn't look at Jordan.

Judge Bennett adjourns for lunch. Frank, Lucy, and Sean walk back to the office. It's two blocks but seems longer when it's 105. Frank is relieved Jordan is eating with his folks. No one talks until they feel the air conditioning.

"Great job," Sean smiles. "Your cross was brilliant."

"Her comment about never trusting men," Lucy says. "I've known abused girls and that's the truth. One night for the man can ruin a girl's life."

"Thanks for that Lucy." Frank shakes his head. "Hope the jurors don't think that way. If I put Jordan on and he comes across as a rich fraternity boy walking away from the harm he's done, we're toast. But if he just sits there, not telling his side of the story, we're probably toast too. What do you guys think? Have I done enough damage to the state's case that I can argue reasonable doubt or do I have to put Jordan on?"

"That's a hard one," says Sean. "Even if the jurors believe Abby said 'no,' with the drinking, the loud music and the making out, the state might have a hard time convincing the jury Jordan heard her and went ahead anyway. Abby came across pretty strong but all we need is one juror who didn't believe her. I've been watching, Juror 8, Mrs. McGonigle, looks skeptical."

"Yeah, I think we got Mrs. McGonigle. Thought so during jury selection. Lucy?"

"I've come to like Jordan. I feel sorry for him. But men get carried away. If he honestly didn't know Abby wasn't consenting I think he would want to get up and say so."

"Great, arguments both ways. Time to get back."

Judge Bennett: Ms. Knowles, does the State rest?

Sandra: Yes, Your Honor.

Judge Bennett: Mr. Perez, do you want to call any witnesses?

The moment of truth. The Rubicon. Frank hesitates.

Judge Bennett: Mr. Perez? Does the defense rest or do you have any witnesses?

Frank: Yes, Your Honor. The defense calls Jordan Nash.

Jordan does better than Frank expected. He comes across as a young, honest college student. Looking directly at the jury, as instructed, he swears he would never force Abby to do anything she didn't want to. "I like her."

As to lying to the police, Jordan said it was the middle of the night, he was scared and had never dealt with the police before.

The cross is brief.

Sandra: Jordan, you've never dealt with the police before? Didn't you have to deal with them when you were arrested for drunk driving?

Jordan looks down and doesn't answer.

Sandra: When you're in trouble you lie, isn't that right? No need to answer that. The jury already knows. Do you agree with your fraternity brothers that when a girl says no she probably doesn't mean it?

Frank: Objection . Argumentative, irrelevant, assuming facts not in evidence. Ms. Knowles knows better.

Judge Bennett: Sustained. You know better, Ms. Knowles.

Sandra: Thank you, your honor. Nothing further.

And that's all folks. Waiting for a verdict isn't "Ladies and Gentlemen, we'll be making an emergency landing," but it's close.

CHAPTER THIRTY

After five hours of deliberation the jury sends a note they are deadlocked. Judge Bennett brings them in and tells them to come back in the morning and try again. Judges hate to declare a mistrial — retrials are expensive, tie up courts, and ruin golf dates. When it becomes clear the jury will never agree Bennett declares a mistrial. Time to start over. A hung jury allows a do-over; double jeopardy doesn't attach unless there is a conviction or an acquittal.

The jurors are excused. While the judge schedules a future hearing, Lucy leaves to talk to the jurors. Six to two guilty. One holdout was an elderly woman who was adamant "She asked for it, what with her dress, should I say undress and getting on the bed with him." The other was a middle-aged man whose niece had been brutally raped when a masked man came through her window with a knife. "That guy was convicted of sexual assault. Jordan didn't threaten her, didn't hurt her, didn't run away. Whatever he did, it wasn't rape."

Mrs. McGonigle?

She led the "he's guilty" crowd. So much for intuition.

Busy catching up with other cases and wanting to give Sandra a chance to cool down, Frank waits a few days to call. "Hi, Frank Perez, how's my favorite prosecutor?" Friendly yet confident, he sits behind his desk, fiddling with a pencil. Behind him on the credenza are pictures of Marie, Frank Junior, and Lilly, school pictures, kids in soccer garb, and on the wall a painting of Don Quixote and Sancho Panza riding out to do justice. He and Marie saw the original painting on their honeymoon in Paris. He has seen *Man of La*

Mancha three times and knows all the words to "reach the unreachable star."

"We're retrying it."

"You're kidding, Sandy. You'll never get any jury to convict. You'll have to get rid of every woman with standards."

"Your guy got lucky. This office is committed to fighting sexual assault."

"Are you sure it doesn't have anything to do with your boss seeking reelection? Doesn't want it getting out her office dismissed a sexual assault case."

"If he pleads we'll recommend the minimum sentence."

"Come on, Sandy, first of all, you know we have a good shot at a hung jury and no way you'll try it a third time. You'll have to explain your failure to Abby and her family."

"Now that I know your defense we have a good shot at a conviction."

"Do you really think Jordan should go to prison and have his life ruined? I've gotten to know him. He's a good kid and you put the fear of God in him. No way will he repeat and you don't need to send a message to warn others; his fraternity brothers saw him taken out in handcuffs. I think he'll plead to simple assault."

Sandra is quiet for what seems a long time. "I don't want Abby to have to go through another trial, and I've got a three-week drug-conspiracy trial set to begin next week. I'll run simple assault by my boss—with jail time."

Frank knows how things work at the DA's. He'll get the deal. Thumbs up to Don Quixote.

"I'll check with Jordan to see if he will plead. He's coming in today. I'll let you know."

Frank returns to a personal injury case. How much should he ask for? Car totaled, several nights in the hospital, no permanent injuries, a month's lost work. It's a pretty strong case and he thinks he'll get a judgment of around $150,000. His contingency fee is a third, a good payday. But even if he gets less he hopes the case settles. He recalls a professor's wise words, "Your case is always worse than you think," and something his Aunt Sally told him.

"I was on a jury and we gave her $75,000. You'd think she'd be happy but I heard her talking with a friend. 'I should never have sued. It was terrible, I can't sleep. I had to sit there for three days with the other lawyer calling me a liar and arguing I was faking it. In cross-examination he brought up stuff I didn't remember and made me look like a fool.' "

Good doctors advise patients to avoid the hospital good lawyers advise clients to avoid the courthouse.

Cindy buzzes. "Jordan and his parents are here."

Shit, his dad. "Send them in."

"Great job, Frank." Paul grabs his hand and shakes it with the strong grip of a winner.

"It wasn't close. Six voted guilty, only two not guilty. We have to have a serious talk about pleading to a reduced charge."

"Bullshit. No plea. She's lying."

"Be quiet, dear," says Jordan's mother, "this is between your son and Frank. We probably shouldn't be here."

"Don't 'dear' me. I'm paying the bill."

"Dad, Mom's right. Stop trashing Abby. I've got to make this decision myself. I'm not a kid." He pauses, "And your being here won't help."

His mother stands to leave. "Paul, I'll wait in the car . . . *Dear*."

Paul, not used to that, grabs his briefcase and leaves. On his way out, "Frank, remember there're other fish in the pond."

"Jordan, your dad's not much on metaphor but he's concerned for you. You have to cut him some slack. I'll grant you he does have a quick temper. You should see him when he misses a putt."

"Easy for you to say. Glad Mom is standing up to him. Finally. Maybe something good will come of this."

"The prosecutor made us an offer—simple assault, a misdemeanor, not sexual assault, which is more serious and a felony. No prison, but some time in county jail. You won't have to register as a sex offender. If you have to register, wherever you live neighbors can go on the web, see you're a sex offender, and think you're a child molester."

"Jail?"

"Probably six months in county and probation for a couple years with monthly reporting."

"I can't do jail time. The one night I spent there was the worst in my life. I can't do a hundred and eighty days."

Frank shakes his head.

It's a good deal. Clients always think they deserve less. I offered a guy ninety days in jail to clear two cases, one a possession of pot and the other cocaine. Tiny amounts. He refused the deal even though there was no possible defense. And he had a prior felony which meant mandatory prison time. His lawyer begged him to plead. So did the judge. He went to trial, lost, and got seven years.

"Jordan, six months is better than ten years. You'll get work release or time off to go to classes. You'll be in a unit with people doing county time. Large rooms with bunk beds."

"What should I do?"

"It's your decision. If we reject the offer they'll retry the sexual assault. Six of the jurors would have convicted you—the two holdouts, luck of the draw. Don't know if we'll get lucky again. And both you and Abby will have to live through another trial."

"I've done enough harm. I'll plead."

CHAPTER THIRTY-ONE

After a couple months at her new job Lucy misses her PD friends. All week she's been hoping to have lunch with them. Several years ago a couple lawyers picked a restaurant for each day of the week. If someone was in trial or had been at the jail, they didn't have to waste time going back to the office to find out where everyone went. This was, of course, the pre-cell phone era. They never changed the restaurant, no matter how much the more fussy lawyers complained, unless someone got food poisoning, they saw more than two roaches on the same day, or the place went bankrupt.

Today, *La Cantina*. Lucy's thankful the menu doesn't list calories, she orders a taco salad and iced tea. Old friends, new gossip. Eight people squeezed into a table for six. All talk at once.

"Hey, Lucy, I heard Sean got a heavy-duty drug case dismissed. Way to go."

I can never admit to this crowd I wish he'd lost.

"Bad search. The cops threatened Jesus that unless he gave up the dealer, they would have ICE send him deep into Mexico and he would never see his family again. And Jesus was an American citizen."

"Fuckers."

"The stupid cops assumed because he was Mexican he must be illegal."

"Send the cops' names so we can look out for them."

Amir, the office intellectual, jumps into the fray, "Corrupt cops remind me of a book I'm reading about Thurgood Marshall. When he was young Marshall worked for the NAACP. Three people were murdered in Oklahoma, an innocent black man was arrested and beaten until he confessed. The cops denied hurting him."

Amir bites into a taco, chews slowly. He has their attention.

Russo, the group jokester, asks, "What happened? I don't have time to read books and I fall asleep in movies."

"Don't worry," says one of the women, "they'll have the Dr. Suess edition soon." Several laugh.

"At the trial the defendant looked at the DA who was questioning him and said, 'The only reason I confessed is that the cops and you were beating me with a hose.' The DA adamantly denied beating him, but when it became clear he couldn't get the defendant to back down, he blurted out, 'You ungrateful nigger, I may have beaten you, but you'd have been dead if I didn't make the cops lay off.'"

"Sounds like a Perry Mason moment."

"Well, they shoot blacks now. Not much improvement," Randy, the office radical, says.

"Read the book. Everyone, even the white folks, knew he was framed. The jury convicted him, but since they knew he was innocent, gave him life instead of death."

"Way cool to be in the same profession as Thurgood Marshall," says Josh, new to the office and yet to be infected with cynicism.

The group breaks into conversations. Cases, judges, prosecutors, but mostly, "Have you heard about . . ." and "Whatever happened to . . ."

Most of the talk stops when Lisa walks in. Lucy hasn't seen her since her going away party when she rescued her from Mr. Sleaze. She's one of the office stars, consistently wins more trials than anyone. Tough ones. She's petite, with long brown hair she wears down unless she's in trial, then in a high ponytail. She passes easily for a college student. "Her looks explain her successes" her male colleagues joke but secretly believe. Too threatening to think she's a better trial lawyer.

"What brings you here? Never seen you eat during trial."

"I've never seen her eat even when she's not in trial."

Lisa waits till the laughter dies down. Whether in trial or at lunch she knows how to hold the crowd's attention. "My client pleaded to a reduced charge after opening statements. A smart thing to do. As we walked out of the courtroom one of the jurors came up to my client, put his hand on his shoulder, and said, 'Good choice, son.' "

Laughter. A couple guys pull over another table. Art, who knows all the gossip, is eager to share. "Did you hear Judge Andrews told a lawyer he'd acquit her client if she took off her shirt?"

"Yeah, that's the Honorable Judge William Bryan Andrews, *the third*."

"She who?"

Art plays it for all it's worth. "You know I don't like to gossip, especially when it's embarrassing and personal."

"Bullshit," several laugh.

"But, if you promise not to tell," he turns to his audience, "Maggie."

"Maggie? Not worth it. He should have asked Jeannie. Miss Wet Dream."

Laughter.

Jesus, it's tough being a woman. Jeannie's terrific. Just because she has huge boobs she shouldn't have to put up with being talked about like that. But if I bring her up, the guys will spend the next fifteen minutes talking about her boobs and boobs in general, and I'll come across as a militant feminist.

She says nothing. Danny walks in.

"Hey Danny, how goes the trial?"

"Same old, same old. Everyone hates me the prosecutor, the judge, the jury, the press, and even my fucking client. Killed his girl-friend—tied her up, forced an orange into her mouth, and locked her in a closet where she died a horrible death—but his only worry is not getting fresh fruit in prison. He's pissed because only Hasidic Jews get fresh fruit as part of their religious diet."

"So why doesn't he claim to be one?"

"He tried on his last visit. He flunked the 'I am a Jew' test, written by a rabbi. Old testament stuff. The downside, if you pass, you get only Kosher, and there isn't a lot of choice."

"I'm surprised there are Hasidic Jews in jail," says Dave. "My people are savvy enough to commit federal crimes, like insider trading, so they end up in fancy federal prisons."

"Come on, Dave. Get over that chosen people rhetoric. Jews are the same as everyone else — they steal, they rob, they murder," says Lisa. "And don't fool yourself. Even federal prisons suck. No name, just a number, no conjugal visits, except those from your cellmate, no friends or family, not to mention shitty food."

Dave continues as if no one had interrupted. "A couple years ago I defended a white supremacist. Hated Jews, but was happy when he got one for a lawyer."

"Yeah, get me out of jail and then I'll kill you," Danny adds.

I love these funny, committed people. If things don't work out maybe I can get a job with them. But not in trials. And not in appeals, if Clay's there. I could work in juvie, less contentious, no juries, the prosecutors mostly committed to helping, not punishing.

Art, having exhausted his stories of sexual encounters at the courthouse, turns to Lucy. "So how's Perez and O'Grady? Working you to death?"

"Doing mostly elder law."

Sensing a possible rumor, Art, perhaps thinking of himself, asks, "So how is it dealing with dirty old men? They hit on you?"

"Not as much as young ones," Lucy says and, perhaps thinking of Art, adds "and they're easier to outrun."

CHAPTER THIRTY-TWO

Lucy is researching a difficult point of law and is more than happy when Cindy buzzes, "Call on line two."

"Hi, I'm Ted Miller, the program director of Our Savior's Methodist Church. One of our parishioners, Jerry Smith, says you represented his mom and are a terrific lawyer. I'm looking for a speaker a week from next Sunday. Do you think you could come and give an after-sermon talk on elder law?"

"Jerry's a grand guy. But I'm not a good speaker and I'm new at the game. Don't know much about the taxation of trusts or Roth IRAs."

"We're a very forgiving group," Ted laughs. "Maybe not the nuts and bolts, but you could talk about the need to prepare for possible disability, that sort of thing."

I know enough about those things and the time has come to get over my fear of public speaking. I'm a lawyer. I quit using drugs. It'll be good to catch up with Jerry.

"Happy to."

The next weeks she frets.

Maybe I shouldn't have agreed. Talking about end of life won't be easy. Sean says I should open with a joke: Voltaire, on his death bed, is asked by a priest to denounce the devil, says, now isn't the best time to make enemies. Not good for a church.

The day arrives. Lucy has a script and gets there early. She catches the last of the sermon. The minister talks slow, repeats his main points, and sometimes he speaks louder, sometimes softer. He talks about playing poker and, if you're losing, you might want to push all your chips in, go all in, and have faith. He closes with "Same with religion."

Service over. The adjacent room has chairs for about forty. Jerry wishes her luck and introduces her.

I'll never be as good as the minister, but hell, I'm all in.

"I'm going to talk about discussing end-of-life issues with your family. It's a tough topic and we're all in denial about mortality. Woody Allen said he didn't mind the idea of dying but he didn't want to be there when it happened."

Silence. A couple of coughs. The older woman in the front row smiles, probably out of kindness.

Fuck Sean. I'm all in.

"Thinking about end of life will make you more comfortable with death. Countless religious leaders, philosophers, novelists, and even Morrie, in t*uesdays with Morrie*, tell us if you can overcome your fear of death, your life gets much better."

It's been a long time since Lucy's been to any church and has only the vaguest idea of how the Lutherans, Baptists, Methodists, or the New Age Church differ. She knows Luther played a big role in the Reformation, which, she learned, was a good thing; that the Catholic Church is in the midst of a disgusting sexual scandal; that the New Age Church has guitar music; and that Evangelists vote Republican.

As a child she went to Sunday School with Jane, her best friend for life, they pinky sweared forever, blood sisters.

I wonder what happened to her. I miss her, our sleepovers, our secret club. We should have let Hazel in. We were horrible.

Since fourth grade the closest she came to a church was a Quaker Meeting. She went with her aunt. At first it was uncomfortable, sitting in a circle, with strangers, no one saying anything. Time passed, alone with her thoughts, and then came comfort and trust, the people around the circle no longer seemed like strangers.

"I'm going to talk about the elephant in the room. When a family member gets old everyone thinks about possible disability, nursing homes, home care, medical treatment, death, funerals, and what's going to happen to them when a parent dies. But most families don't talk about these things. What's even more verboten?"

She pauses, looks at the confused audience.

"Dirty jokes."

This gets a laugh.

"But I won't be telling any."

From the back of the room, "Darn." The ice has been broken. Lucy realizes she can do this. The audience becomes hers. About thirty folks, dressed in Tucson casual, church clothes are way too hot when it's 107 degrees, mostly older, a couple of mothers with babies, some drinking coffee, others eating donuts. Lucy had been offered both, but fearful of spills or food on her face, declined.

To hell with the script. I'll talk about what matters.

"I never talked to my mother about her fear of dying and my fear of a future without her. I will always regret it. You don't have to go through that.

"Let me tell you something wonderful. Hearing is the last thing to go. A friend's mother was dying and we visited her in hospice. She was in her last days. Not moving, eyes closed. All seemed lost. Her husband started talking about trips they had made to France, about shows they had seen in New York, about Christmases with the grandkids, and then he bent low and whispered, 'Dear, it's OK for you to go. We love you and we'll be fine.' "

Silent nods.

"A few weeks ago I was called to the hospital. Edith, my amazing eighty-year-old client, was on life support. Her Living Will said she didn't want extraordinary procedures to keep her alive, but the doctors weren't going to stop treating her unless the family agreed. They didn't. It got nasty. The sister accusing her brother of wanting to keep their mom alive because he felt guilty about moving to Chicago, and the brother accusing her of wanting to pull the plug to save money.

"Fortunately she had a Health Care Power of Attorney. She hadn't appointed either of her children as her agent but rather a niece, Jessica. I met Jessica at the ER. We talked to the family and the doctors. Jessica decided to take her aunt off life support. I can't imagine how hard it was on Jessica. But it was the right decision."

But who knows? Edith, a wonderful woman, a compassionate and loving woman, did not go peacefully into that good night, she struggled for life. Pulling the plug isn't turning off the light.

A question brings Lucy back to the present.

"What if you want to give money to your grandchildren, but fear they'll use it for tattoos and nose rings?" asks a woman in the front row. She had followed every word. Folks like her make speakers better.

Lucy nods and laughs. "Set up a trust that will delay gifts or provide that the funds can only be used for education. Removing the tattoos is their problem."

She gets back on script and assures her audience that once families start talking there is often closeness and humor.

"Most family fights aren't about money but about family heirlooms."

A woman in the back who had been staring at Lucy raises her hand.

She probably thinks this has been a waste of time and wants to talk about Roth IRAs.

"When my three daughters were young they all loved my mom's dolls. She called them together, took out her dolls one by one, and told each of them who was to get which one. We had a good cry after that."

Lucy can't talk. She sees the three young girls, the grandmother, and the dolls. Thankfully the minister stands.

"Thank you, Lucy, this has been wonderful. Jerry was right. You've given us so much to think about and when we talk to our families we'll go all in."

Back at the office on Monday Lucy reports to Frank. "I think I've done good. The audience was great. Several came up to me, thanked me, and shared some of their experiences. A few asked for my card. Two couples are coming in tomorrow."

"New clients," laughs Frank, "best part of pro bono."

"Remember Jerry, Mary Smith's son? He's the one who

recommended me."

"How's his mom?"

"Hanging in. She came home. Some people do. Loves her granddaughter. I was surprised how accepting everyone was of Jerry, Alan, and their baby."

"Lucy, you should go to church every now and then. Learn something about your future clients. Us believers aren't all stuck in the Middle Ages."

CHAPTER THIRTY-THREE

Frank invites Lucy for Saturday night dinner. She assumes he included the whole office, but when she asks him, Frank says, "Just you, I want you to meet Marie and the kids."

Lucy chides herself for being nervous.

It's not like I'm having dinner with a judge or the mayor. What should I wear? Frank has a couple young kids. I've seen their pictures. I'm glad he doesn't talk about them every day like some people I know who think their baby is the next Einstein or Michelle Obama.

She settles on jeans and a multicolored tunic.

The drive to Frank's house takes less time than she or her GPS figured. She locates the house but doesn't stop. She'd noticed a burger place a few blocks away and drives into the parking lot. Her mom had drummed into her to never show up early. How many times had she heard about her dad's sister, who always came before they were ready? They were still in pj's or hadn't finished cooking. Always threw them off schedule.

She takes out her phone, checks Facebook, reads a news story about how the Supreme Court, like every other institution, is less collegial. Finally time to go.

Frank lives in the south-side barrio in an area filled with small houses. Most of the yards are attractively landscaped with desert flowers and cactus. A few aren't, front yards filled with discarded appliances, dead plants, and old cars rusting on blocks.

Before Lucy can ring the bell, Marie opens the door, "Hi, come on in. I'd apologize for the toys and clutter, but when you have two kids under ten there's not much you can do."

Lucy's surprised how attractive Marie is. The pictures in Frank's office don't do her justice. She has flawless brown skin, big brown eyes, and shiny black hair that falls in waves past her shoulders. Marie's casually dressed in jeans and a T-shirt that reads, *Certified Book Addict.*

Mine would say, Certified Drug Addict.

"Frank, Lucy's here," Marie calls. "He's watching soccer in the bedroom with the kids. I'm not a fan."

Frank walks in also dressed casually in jeans, a polo shirt, and flip-flops. Lucy is glad she didn't overdo it.

"Have you met the kids yet?" A boy, a girl, a mixed-breed brown dog. "Lilly's eight and Frank, who we call Junior, is six."

"Glad to meet you," Lucy says.

Glad to meet you? I'm such an idiot. They're kids, not colleagues. At least I didn't try to shake their hands or ask for their business cards.

"Hi," Lilly bends to pet the dog. "This is our dog, Sparkie. She's four in people years. You can pet her. She's friendly."

The boy smiles, but says nothing.

Lucy, who is more comfortable with dogs than children, pets Sparkie.

"I have a dog named Teddy."

"How old is he?" asks Lilly.

"I'm not exactly sure. Teddy's a rescue. About four."

"People or dog years?" asks Junior.

"People years."

Lucy hasn't thought much about having kids. Most of her friends are more interested in careers than motherhood. Being pregnant seems like a nightmare—nausea, getting fatter and fatter. Throwing up. Maybe she should think about being in a committed relationship before she thinks about having babies.

Clay?

"Dinner's ready," Marie says. Lucy follows them into the dining room. It's not large, the wooden table and chairs take up most of the room. The walls are decorated with the kids' drawings. The table is loaded with colorful serving bowls filled with enchiladas, beans, Spanish rice, and salad.

"We're informal here. Take what you want. The enchiladas are cheese and sour cream." Lucy digs in. Sparkie, in her crate in the kitchen, whines.

"Sparkie wants food, but we don't give her table scraps."

Frank, who does, looks down. Says nothing.

"Frank tells me you're an English teacher," says Lucy. "Where do you teach?"

"Tucson High. American and Mexican lit."

"Must be a lot of preparation."

"Yeah, but I love to read."

"I'm reading the *Hobbit*," says Lilly.

"I read that," says Lucy, "but I was in junior high."

"My teacher says I read above grade level."

"Show-off."

"Kids." Marie gives them the knock-it-off look and passes the enchiladas. "Have some more, Lucy. There's plenty."

Lucy takes another enchilada. She hasn't been around young kids much. She ventures a question.

"What are you reading, Junior?"

"I don't like to read, I like video games."

Wrong question.

"My mom's a great teacher," says Lilly. "The kids give her mugs that say, 'Greatest Teacher' and she was Teacher of the Year."

Marie can do everything.

Lucy tries again. "We have a dog at our office."

"Dad told me that," says Lilly. "His name is Sean and he's a Golden Retriever."

"You're wrong, his name is Dusty. You don't know everything," says Junior.

Should I explain that Dusty is Sean's dog? Nah, too complicated.

Frank comes to the rescue. "Sean's my law partner, you've met him. Dusty is his dog, but he brings him to the office most days."

"Where does he pee?" asks Junior.

"Good question. He goes out in the back yard like your dog." Lucy's making progress.

Junior, pleased with both the compliment and answer, asks "How old is he in dog years?"

"I don't know but he barks above his grade level."

Bingo.

Junior takes another enchilada. "Do you work with my Dad?" Lilly asks.

"I do."

"Is he bossy like here?" Junior asks.

Everything is comfortable and happy. How can Marie cook a terrific meal, teach full time, and raise kids as well as being a wife?

When everyone is finished the kids take their plates into the kitchen and disappear into another room. Frank follows them. "I promised to help Junior with his reading."

"Lucy, want to help with the dishes?"

The two go into the kitchen. "I'll rinse. You can put them in the dishwasher."

"Your kids are adorable."

Marie smiles.

Dinner was more pleasant than I expected. Kids are great. Why not ask?

"Isn't it difficult to have a career and raise kids?"

Marie doesn't answer immediately. Lucy wonders if she's blundered into too personal a question.

"It's a hard question to answer. The hardest part was getting Frank on board. He assumed I'd stay home with the kids like our moms. But the kids are doing great and I love teaching."

"How can you do everything?"

"A cleaning lady." Lucy smiles. "It's worth every penny."

"I'll remember that."

"Don't get me wrong. It's a lot of work to do both. Sometimes there's a school event that conflicts with something they want me at, like a soccer game."

"Must be tough."

"It's easier for teachers to balance family and career. We get most holidays and summer off. And unlike women lawyers, we're not the new kids on the block and don't have to prove to the boys we belong."

"Things are getting a little better. A classmate of mine just became the first woman partner in a big Phoenix firm."

"You want to do that?"

"No way. She has to bill twenty-four hundred hours a year, about sixty hours a week with no vacations."

"No vacations save money. Frank promised me his practice won't get in the way of his family. Thus far, so good. He tells me there were only a dozen or so women in his class of over a hundred. Now half of his trial practice class are women. But I guess they still have a hard time breaking in, being the new kids."

"The same thing with men who want to teach elementary school or be nurses."

"Good point. And any man who wants to teach in elementary school is viewed with suspicion."

"My third-grade teacher was a man. He changed my life, convinced me I was smart. It's amazing how one person can do that."

"Yeah, every now and then I have to remind myself that I'm not just discussing novels. Let's go find Frank."

CHAPTER THIRTY-FOUR

Bobby-Jo's in line when Lucy arrives. They had agreed to meet at five in hopes of beating the crowd. Sauce has good food, casual atmosphere, beer, and wine. It appeals to the university crowd and is always busy.

"Am I'm late?" Lucy asks.

"No, I got here a minute ago."

At their weekly lunch they take turns picking a pizza to share. Lucy's turn, so it's thin crust, pepperoni, and mushroom. Lucy adds a small green salad. Bobby-Jo, a cup of tomato soup.

"Let's get a table on the patio. I brought Teddy," Lucy says.

"Good, it's quieter out there."

Bobby-Jo makes a fuss over Teddy. Lucy gives him a bone.

Lucy's glad to be away from the constant ringing of the phones and the busy pace of the office. She hopes the patio will stay empty.

"How's Perez and O'Grady?"

"Things are going well. It's taken me a little time to feel comfortable with Sean. Weird sense of humor. I think he has a drinking problem. Frank's likable, easy to get along with. I'm lucky to have them as my bosses. I've had way worse."

"The hot chick at the front desk, what's her story?"

"Cindy? She's technically the secretary, receptionist. But she's way more than that. She's worked in law offices a long time, knows a lot."

"And she's gorgeous."

"Don't get your hopes up. She's straight, and half the men in Tucson are hot for her. I think Sean and her have some history."

"Cause problems?"

"Cindy's always professional. Sean sometimes says inappropriate stuff but no more to Cindy than anyone else."

Lucy opens her tote bag. Takes out a bowl and pours water for Teddy.

"How are things with Clay?"

"Good. I'm not sure he totally trusts me, but I think he's getting there. We've been closer since I told him the truth."

"It's hard to tell people you're an addict, even a recovered one. I was terrified to tell people I was a lesbian. I thought they'd shun me. A few did, but mostly it was, 'Duh, we figured that.' "

"Funny," laughs Lucy. "Not sure they'd feel the same way about drugs."

Bobby-Jo puts a slice of pizza on each of their plates.

"Smells good," says Lucy. "But I'm finishing my salad first."

"I'll leave you some."

"Better for me if you don't."

Two young women smile at Teddy. "Can we pet him? He's adorable."

"Sure." The women rub his ears. Teddy rolls over and taking the hint they give him a tummy rub. Lucy loves this almost as much as Teddy.

"What have you and Bridget got planned for the weekend?" Lucy asks.

"Nothing."

"Nothing? That doesn't sound like you two."

"We broke up," says Bobby-Jo.

Broke up? So lesbians have the same problems? Maybe I should counsel her. That would be a change.

"Why didn't you tell me?"

"It just happened."

"You don't seem upset."

"I'm not sure how I feel."

Confused as the rest of us.

"I'm not surprised it's over. You've been together, what six, seven months? Almost a record."

"Very funny, Lucy. I don't want to control my girlfriends' lives. But I have one rule: no drugs or alcohol in my house. A couple weeks ago she wound up in the ER. Too much marijuana candy."

"Pot candy? I didn't think eating it was anymore dangerous than smoking it."

"It's way stronger than smoking. People think it's harmless, so they eat too much. Have you ever been in one of the dispensaries selling medical pot? They look like a candy store: chocolate bars, gummy bears, and lollipops. All kinds of candy, but pot infused."

"Is that why you broke up?"

Bobby-Jo nods. "That and when I found some of the candy in the fridge. I asked her to leave, she said, she would, but she didn't."

"Can I get you anything?" the server asks. Both shake their heads.

"Too dangerous for me to have drugs around. When she was at the gym, I gathered all her stuff and put it in garbage bags outside the door. She didn't have much."

"What happened when she got home?"

"She threw a fit. Accused me of stealing her money. Not that she had any. Said she'd get even. She's probably bluffing. It's my problem. I'll take care of it. Enough about me. You didn't finishing telling me about your love life."

"Not much else to say. We spend weekends together, but rarely weeknights. I like to get dressed at my house. Clay likes his because it's closer to the office. We've discussed living together once or twice. I hope it happens. I'm glad I didn't ruin it."

"I'd like to meet him."

A group of college girls find seats on the patio. All have long blonde hair and wear short shorts. Lucy looks at Bobby-Jo, who is checking them out. "Can I ask you a question—about being gay?"

"You thinking about joining my team?"

Lucy chuckles. "Probably a stupid question, but did you decide one day to be gay or were you born that way? Some women seem to choose being lesbian."

"Queer the moment I came out of the womb. I didn't know it. I just knew I was different from other girls."

Teddy barks. He's looking at a small white dog in a car. Lucy distracts him with one of the treats she always carries.

"It took me a long time to admit I was different, even to myself. In church all I heard was 'homosexuality is a sin.' My mom and everyone in town believed that. I believed it. I studied the girls around me. Mimicked how they acted. I had to learn to walk like a girl, talk like a girl, and giggle like a girl. I pretended I had crushes on boys. The good news is none of them reciprocated."

"Ha," Lucy laughs. "In high school I was the cover girlfriend for a gay friend. He had to keep saying he liked my ass."

"I always had a suspicion about one couple in high school. Anyway, how goes the law?"

"I want to do elder law but I'm not sure they want to go in that direction. I hate trials. You'll love this: I persuaded a grandmother not to cut her son out of the will because he's gay."

"Queers one, bigots zero." They laugh.

Pizza eaten, Lucy refills their drinks.

"I wish all my girls could do as well as you," Bobby-Jo says. "A couple of women in my group relapsed. Could have died. Without Narcan one of them would have. Whatever they took had Fentanyl mixed in. It's so dangerous. Fentanyl kills."

Fentanyl. Harold. I'll get that prick.

Bobby-Jo looks at her watch. "I gotta go. Counseling group, five women, an hour of self-doubt, domestic violence, childhood trauma, and the thrill of using. I don't have to tell you."

She gets up. They hug.

Later that night, after feeding Teddy and telling him what a great dog he is, Lucy goes to bed. She goes to sleep quickly but not peacefully.

Caps and gowns. Pomp and Circumstance. Smiles and excitement.

"We made it."

"All over but the bar exam."

"I got that job."

Music, classmates marching in line, an auditorium filled with family and friends, applause, and suddenly the dean.

"Lucy, you can't graduate, you didn't turn in your final paper."

Panic. Didn't I? This can't be right. I read all those cases, wrote two drafts. Maybe not. Maybe I didn't turn it in. Maybe I can't graduate. Where's everyone gone?

Lucy wakes up. Did that happen?

CHAPTER THIRTY-FIVE

Globe is a small mining town a couple of hours from Tucson and Phoenix and half an hour from the San Carlos Indian Reservation. Its heyday was in the 1910s when it boasted one of the nation's top copper mines. It had a hotel, a bank, a courthouse, and various stores. The entire downtown is now protected as a historic site. The price of copper fell but Globe hung on as a tourist attraction and commercial hub for the reservation and the smaller towns that surround it. Most young folks are leaving for bigger cities, more jobs, and better restaurants, but Globe still boasts two high schools and a four-screen theatre.

Sean grew up in Globe.

Dinner with his family—his parents, his sister Sherry and her "terribly bright" children, Seamus, seven, and Mollie, five. It's his monthly visit. He used to come weekly but you know how things are: bigger city, higher salaries, more restaurants . . .

"Mom, great pasta. You have to give me the recipe."

"I've given it to you at least three times."

The two kids love to see grownups make mistakes. They giggle.

"Well, yes," Sean mumbles. He doesn't cook, he'd asked to be polite. "Pass the salad. How goes the teaching, Mom?"

"Still love it. Have some more pasta, looks like you're losing weight."

"Seamus, stop playing with your food," cautions Sherry.

"Who was that kid in your class you were so proud of? Was it Danny?"

"Danny's doing great. He has a flair for mechanics and got a good job with the Ford Dealership in Scottsdale. He married Marlene, another of my kids. Are you seeing anyone?"

This question started in high school. How's that sweet girl Ellie? You still going out? Mom loved Ellie. We both did. She married that jerk, Peter.

"I've met someone. I'll keep you posted, Mom, no need to keep asking."

"I ran into Ellie last week. Another baby on the way."

"Mom, Seamus kicked me."

"Did not."

"Did too."

"Kids, your uncle is here and if you don't behave no dessert."

"Can we go watch TV?" asks Seamus.

Dad does not share his wife's concerns. "How's business?"

Sean explains the firm is still above water, doing better, and their new hire, Lucy, is working out well but they're not sure if they'll make her a permanent offer.

"How's the teenage boy you guys defended?" asks Sherry. She mouths "the rapist."

Thank god I never told her about Harold.

"What's a rapist?"

"Never you mind, Mollie. Finish your dinner," says her mother.

"Jordan's not doing terrific. He dropped out of college and isn't sure if he'll—"

"Can we go watch TV?" Seamus has no interest in what a rapist is. His interest is in his cartoon show, the one that is tricking him into learning math.

"Don't interrupt your uncle. You can go when Mollie finishes her salad."

"Yuck," whispers Mollie.

"Jordan's a bright kid. His friends dropped him and the university might kick the fraternity off campus."

"Good," says Sherry. Mom nods.

"Is he working?" asks Dad.

"Yeah, he gets out of jail a couple of hours a day to work."

"I ate most of my salad."

Truth be told Sean had secretly taken it off her plate and put it on his own.

The battle is lost, and with a theatrical sweep of her arm, Sherry points to the front room and commands, "Go."

Sean doesn't tell them Frank hired Jordan a couple of days a week to file, run errands, and walk Dusty. Sherry'd be outraged.

"Dad, how's the hardware store? Still worried about Walmart?"

"They're trying to get rezoning to allow box stores. And your father is leading the fight against it."

It's wonderful how proud they are of one another. Of course, it wasn't always that way. There were fights about the new car and why didn't dad do more around the house.

"It will ruin our little city," Dad shakes his head. "They're bringing in some big guns, expensive law firms from Phoenix. All we can afford is your old buddy, Eddie."

"Eddie? He's a good lawyer. I'll see him while I'm here. Maybe I can help."

"Seamus won't let me watch my show," says Mollie as she returns. "Uncle Sean, will you read to us before you go?"

"Sure. As always," says Sean. "Isn't Globe too small for Walmart?"

"Walmart knows this place will grow. Young people are moving in, they can work from home and the commute isn't as bad as the 405 in LA. Besides, unlike the schools in big cities, our schools are mixed: whites, blacks, Hispanics, and Indians."

"Indians are now called 'Native Americans,' dear."

Ignoring this constant correction Dad continues. "You know an Indian from San Carlos playing for your old high school scored a career high of over three thousand points, putting him right up there with Mike Bibby who played pro. You know Bibby, the African American."

"Bibby played for Arizona in l997 when they beat Duke for the national championship."

Sean almost has to shout over the TV lesson. "If half the ducks left and two came back how many ducks would there be?"

"Turn the TV down." The kids listen to him.

Seamus does. The grownups will never know how many ducks there would have been.

"In high school you had that stupid band, what? The Nerds? The Thoughtful Nerds? Total embarrassment. Pretty much ruined my prom." Sherry's words are harsh but her tone forgiving. She loves her brother and the prom worked out; she met her husband.

The band wasn't bad . . . if only they had let me be lead guitar. And if we had a good singer. And better drummer. The Beatles would never have gone anywhere without Ringo.

"You ever regret not working at juvenile court and no longer working with kids?" asks Mom.

Sean shrugs, "You know me, I regret everything. Even Ellie sometimes."

"You know one of your heroes, Gault, is from Globe," says Sherry, who is convinced, like her Mom, Sean should've stayed in juvenile court.

"Of course I know that. I probably sat in the same chair he did in civics." He recalls Mr. Gross, his favorite teacher, telling the story of Gault.

On June 8, 1964, Globe's sheriff arrested Gerald Gault, a poor fifteen-year-old, for making a lewd phone call. He denied doing it. The juvenile court judge, finding him "delinquent," ordered him confined in the State Industrial School until he was twenty-one. Had Gerald been an adult the maximum sentence he could have served was two months. In a famous case, *In Re Gault,* the Supreme Court reversed the decision, finding that he was denied due process and now juveniles have rights Gerald never did: to a lawyer, to be informed of the charges against them, and to confront witnesses against them.

"I remember talking about the case in class. One kid said the lesson was not to make lewd phone calls, but someone corrected him by pointing out we can't because our phone numbers show. I thought, 'Wow, a poor kid who sat in this room went to the United States Supreme Court and changed American law.' So sister dear, I used to be an idealist."

"Good for you," says Sherry. "Kids turn off the TV and Sean will read you a story."

"In light of Walmart," says Sean, "I'll make it *Where the Wild Things Are.* They gnashed their terrible teeth."

CHAPTER THIRTY-SIX

Even though she'd sworn off criminal cases Lucy agreed to take Karen's. Somehow Karen reminded her of herself. Maybe she could help her.

She met Karen at the Serenity Fundraiser. She thinks Joyce introduced them, but she isn't sure. All she recalled was Karen wore a heavy wool sweater—way too warm for the season.

Karen set up an appointment. She's attractive, olive-skinned, slim, with dark, curly hair in need of a cut. Lucy guesses late twenties, early thirties. No visible tattoos or piercings. Hoop earrings. Either Latina or mixed race. Again, too warm a day for a sweater.

Hope it isn't covering bruises or track marks? No one hides tats anymore.

Before Lucy can say a word, Karen starts complaining about her public defender. "Are those people even lawyers? He's rude, sloppy, and fat. Like really fat. Never calls me back and always in a hurry."

Poor Keith. He's so smart and a great lawyer, but I've never seen him with a date, male or female. He jokes about his weight, but it's like drawing the sting in a trial. Do it before someone else does. I wonder which is worse: being a recovering drug addict or being fat?

"Karen, all the PDs are lawyers and are competent, but if you want to hire us, we'd be happy to have you as a client. Tell me about your case and when I get more information, I'll tell you how much it will cost to defend you."

"I wanna hire you. I want a woman lawyer. My dad can pay whatever. He owes me. Spends a ton of money on his stupid bimbo girlfriend. The bitch is only three years older than me. You'd never guess, even with all the plastic surgery and the boob job and the gaudy expensive clothes he pays for . . ."

Karen runs out of steam, shrugs.

I don't have the slightest clue what to charge her even if I find out more information. Too bad we don't charge by the word.

"I brought along the stuff my 'lawyer' gave me." She hands Lucy what appears to be an indictment, a few pages of police reports, and a lab report.

"Give me a minute to look at this." Lucy starts skimming.

A few minutes later, fidgeting, Karen says, "I'm in rehab at Serenity House. I'm doing great. I'm clean. Does that help?"

Hard to believe she's clean. She's jittery, manic, and that sweater. Withdrawal?

"That's great, Karen. Congratulations. Of course it helps. I need to read this stuff. Give me a few minutes. Get a drink or you can play with our firm dog, Dusty. The kitchen's next door. Dusty usually in there."

"I'm fine. Promise I'll be quiet."

Karen fidgets.

Wrong time, wrong place. Karen had been a passenger in her boyfriend's car when he was stopped by police. Heroin was found in the glove compartment. She's facing a major felony, possession for sale, mandatory prison. Lucy puts down the papers.

"What do you think about my chances of winning?" Karen asks.

"I don't have all the information I need but it's a tough case to win. All the state has to prove is you possessed at least a gram of heroin. They don't have to show you sold any or even tried to. If the heroin weighs a gram or more Arizona law presumes it's for sale and not for personal use."

"We didn't sell any. What do you mean, *pres-umes*?"

Shit, how can I explain this without legal words?

"Think about apples, not heroin. If you had two apples, people would assume you were going to eat them. If you had a hundred apples, people would assume you were going to sell the apples, not eat all one hundred."

I should be able to come up with something better. What if she asks if they were going to give the apples away or make a bunch of pies?

"What if I was going to make pies?" Karen asks.

"Tell me about the drugs."

"The drugs were Dylan's, my boyfriend," says Karen. "Maybe ex-boyfriend."

"Your fingerprints were on the wrapping and you told the cops some of the heroin was yours. Legally that's enough for possession."

"That's what the other lawyer said. He also told me to plead."

"Why did they pull you over?" Lucy asks.

"They say Dylan was speeding, but it's because we're brown."

Lucy lets that pass. She doesn't know what to say.

"Did they give him a breath test or make him do any field sobriety tests?"

"No."

"Do you know if Keith made a motion to throw out the case on the grounds the cop had no reason to stop the car?"

"Yeah. Keith told me the judge ruled against him. He probably screwed it up."

I could defend Keith's work. But why bother.

"Have you ever been arrested before or have any prior convictions?"

Karen hesitates. "I got charged with possession of a pipe. But I took a drug class and it was dismissed."

Lucy's not sure what else to ask. Karen breaks the silence.

"Lucy, do I have to go to trial? I don't want to. I don't want to testify. Will the person that sold us the drugs be there?"

Lucy's thankful she got a question she can answer.

"Don't worry, you don't have to go to trial and if you did, no one can make you testify. The person who sold you the drugs has nothing to do with this case. If you don't want a trial, we have to work on a plea. If you give up the guy who sold you the stuff they may be willing to give you a better deal."

Karen's face suddenly loses all its color and she looks frightened. "No, I would never do that, never. I'd rather go to prison. He'd hurt me, might even kill me. No, don't even talk about it."

"Sorry, Karen, relax. You don't have to tell the prosecutor. You don't have to tell me. Although you do understand anything you tell me is confidential?"

God that's the first thing you should tell a client. I screwed up. Does she even understand what confidentiality means? Well, at least we agree we don't want to go to trial. But I got a new client.

CHAPTER THIRTY-SEVEN

"Lucy, Nancy Delaney, from the county attorney's office calling about the Portillo case," says Cindy.

Nancy Delaney? Sounds familiar. Blonde curly hair, blue eyes, and a smile. How do I know her?

"Hi, Lucy, I'm handling Karen Portillo's case. Good news for your client. We got the criminalist's report back and there isn't enough heroin to charge possession for sale. Just under a gram. We're going to dismiss and refile as simple possession."

Great. I won't have to go to trial. Karen will want to plead. Still a felony, but no prison, probation mandatory. What would Lisa do? Ask for drug court.

"That's great. Any chance you'll agree to drug court if she pleads? Nice girl. She has a misdemeanor possession of drug paraphernalia, which was dismissed. Nothing else. She's clean. Been at Serenity House working hard on her rehab."

"You drive a hard bargain. I'll check her record and if it's clean, I'll make it a drug court available plea."

Me, drive a hard bargain? Who is this Nancy? "Mary Poppins" drives a hard bargain? Maybe their case is falling apart and they know I'm new. Maybe the arresting officer has died. Maybe I have overlooked something. Wait. I remember Nancy.

Nancy was a third year when Lucy started law school. She had talked at first year orientation about the importance of sleep, exercise, getting away from law school now and then. Several speakers had warned how stressful law school would be. They overplayed it. Halfway through first semester the guy sitting next to Lucy in Civil Procedure said, "I haven't had a mental breakdown, I still get along with my wife, I haven't become an alcoholic, I can sleep. What am I doing wrong?"

Lucy blushes, remembers seeing Nancy in the women's bathroom. She got her period, needed a quarter for the Tampax machine. She was frantically rummaging through her purse when Nancy handed her a couple quarters. "I hate when that happens."

By the time Lucy bought the Tampax, went into the bathroom stall to put it in, and came out, Nancy was gone. She had never thanked her.

Maybe Nancy offered the deal because she's decent, cares more about doing the right thing than getting convictions. Lisa tells me there are some DAs like that, but that's not what I heard from the other PDs. Maybe Lisa gets good deals because they're afraid of facing her in trial. I wonder what Clay thinks. I have to get Karen to agree to plead.

"Cindy, I have to run over to Serenity House to see Karen. I might not get back to the office today."

"OK, I'll call you if anything happens you need to know. Are you free for lunch tomorrow?"

Me? Lunch?

"Yes, where do you want to go?"

"How about the salad bar on Sixth?"

"Sounds good. Let's try to go at eleven forty-five and beat the rush."

Lucy wonders what kind of vibes she's putting out. First Delaney offers her a smokin' deal and then Cindy wants to go to lunch. Lucy realizes that Cindy should be in awe of her, not vice versa, but she envies Cindy's good looks, sense of humor, and confidence. And smarts.

Serenity House is located in an old motel that fell on hard times during construction of a new ramp on the interstate. There are thirty beds available for inpatient residents, and they have a larger outpatient program. Women only. The pool has been covered with cement and made into a patio. There's a pleasant dining room decorated with posters of inviting vegetables. The food's healthy and tasty. A few women complain about gaining weight, but all they do is complain. Anyone who's ever dieted knows how hard it is to give up food. When you also have to give up cocaine, heroin, whatever your drug of choice is, it's almost impossible. Far better a donut than meth.

When Lucy was a Serenity House client, the staff instituted a no-smoking policy. Clients were provided free nicotine replacement products like patches, classes on ways to quit cold-turkey, or by slowly cutting down. Several women quit the program. The staff reversed the policy. Quitting smoking is a bridge too far.

Lucy finds Karen in the small library writing in her journal. "Karen, we have to talk."

"I'm not going to prison, am I?"

"No, good news. The county attorney's going to dismiss the sales charge. No prison. Let's talk about your choices."

"I can't go to prison," Karen trembles, " The women at rehab have told me horrible stories of prisoners screaming all night, having to wear used, dirty clothes, fighting, being raped by guards, attacked by other prisoners."

"Listen to me. You're not going to prison. They don't send people to prison for simple possession."

"It wasn't mine. It was Dylan's."

"We talked about that. You said you didn't want to go to trial."

Hope she hasn't changed her mind, but at least if I lose she won't go to prison.

"No, I don't want to go to trial."

"Then you have to plead guilty. You'll get probation. You'd only go to prison if you blow probation. There's another option that's better than straight probation, drug court."

"Drug court?"

"Drug court helps you get clean and stay clean. You have to do drug testing, and go to counseling, which you would also have to do on probation. But in drug court you appear in front of a judge every two weeks. If you successfully complete the drug court program you'll get a misdemeanor instead of a felony."

"Why do I care about a misdemeanor?"

"A felony can ruin your life. It's hard to get a job, even a low-paying one, even an interview. Hard to get a decent place to live, you can't get grants, scholarships, any benefits. You can't vote. Convictions stay with you forever thanks to the internet. Misdemeanors don't cause those problems."

Karen looks confused.

"Karen, I know you're clean now and want to stay that way. It's hard. I've been there. It's easy to take that one little pill or hit. Look what happened to Joyce."

"Will I have to tell who we got the drugs from?"

"No."

"Are you sure? No way can I rat out those guys. I'd rather go to prison."

"I'm sure. Call me in a couple days and let me know if you want to do drug court. But don't wait too long."

"I'll do it," Karen says.

"You're sure?"

She nods her head. "Lucy, I knew you were a great lawyer. Thank you so much."

Why is she so scared of the person who sold them the heroin? Is he part of a cartel? Harold? I'll get him, whatever it takes.

CHAPTER THIRTY-EIGHT

Frank's intro to trial work was rocky. His first case, he prosecuted a DUI, a belligerent young man driving a BMW sports car who tested more than twice the legal limit. Frank lost.

After the trial he talked to one of the jurors and, expecting at worst, faint praise, he let drop, "That was my first trial."

"That's what we thought."

Frank tells that story. He's that kind of guy. Humility has done him good. No one likes stuffed shirts, strutting, looking down on secretaries and plumbers. And it helps being slightly overweight, wearing nice suits, but not too nice, not using big words. He treats jurors as his peers, not pounding the obvious into their heads, often leaving it to them to figure things out. Unlike many of his "learned colleagues" he knows when to shut up.

He was surprised when Professor Fry asked him to teach a section of trial practice. Once law schools were entirely theoretical. Nothing practical like trial practice. It goes back to 1870. Christopher Columbus Langdell became the dean of the Harvard Law School and preached, *"Law is a science and, just as botanists learn their trade in the laboratory, law students will learn lawyering in the library."* One hundred years in the library. Worse than one hundred years of solitude.

Then after decades someone asked, "Where's the courthouse?" Now students not only get the address but tips on what to do when they get there. No one believes law is a science anymore, but that's another story. The ghost of Christopher Columbus Langdell still haunts legal education, but that too is another story.

Professor Fry's evidence class was one of Frank's favorites. He made the class understandable and fun. They were studying the hearsay rule: a witness can testify only to their firsthand knowledge not what someone told them. For example, "Agatha told me the butler did it." Agatha's not there and can't be cross-examined. How does she know he did it? Did she see him do it? Does she have bad eyesight? Bad memory? Does she hate him for his Irish accent? Or did she run out of suspects and the butler was the last one standing?

To illustrate hearsay Professor Fry tells his favorite story.

George takes his dog for a walk and sees a burglar crawl out of a window. His dog gives chase. George can't keep up and loses sight of the man and his dog. A few blocks later he finds his dog barking at a man halfway up a tree. At trial:

George*: The guy in the tree is the burglar my dog chased.*

Defense lawyer*: Objection! Hearsay! The only way he would know that is if the dog told him it was the same guy he chased. The dog's statement would be an out-of-court statement introduced for its truth. How do we know if the dog is being truthful?*

Prosecuting lawyer*: Is my esteemed colleague suggesting that dogs lie?*

Defense lawyer*: Absolutely not. Dogs never lie. But they have a great sense of humor.*

Frank told this story to Marie and she loved it. Now if Sparkie does something wrong, she says, "He's not a bad dog but has a great sense of humor."

Trial practice: twenty students, three hours a week, playing lawyer, trying murder cases. Lawyering comes alive. Should I have objected to that question? Should I have put that witness on first? How did that witness get away from me on cross?

When students get their first case, it's, "Damn, we can never win." After many hours in the library reading cases, it's "We can't lose." Then the trial. Cursing on the inside they sit calmly watching their opponents, who they thought were their friends, brilliantly tear apart all they had created.

But their turn will come.

Welcome to the adversary system.

The semester ends with a trial with family and friends as jurors. Frank's invited to the post-trial party at a local watering hole. Spirits are high, they survived.

The smell of spilled beer, french fries, bratwurst, and sawdust. Flashing Bud Light signs compete with those of Miller and Tecate. On the wall a flat screen TV silently plays *High Noon*. With "Do not forsake me on this our wedding day" running through his head, Frank takes a seat where he can see the gunfight, one of his favorites.

"Phil, you're a hell of a prosecutor, even your mother voted for acquittal."

After a few beers they turn to bitching about the law school. No surprise there, a favorite topic.

Frank grows restless. "No one asked you to come to law school."

"Oh yes they did," says Liana, "I was accepted at other schools, some higher ranked, but Professor Attwell called me, told me how she was looking forward to seeing me in the fall."

"I guess they didn't want you that bad," laughs Anthony, an African American student from Stanford. "The dean called me."

"Well, things have changed since I was a student," offers Frank. "We were thankful we got in and they actually flunked people."

"Did they do the 'look to your left, look to your right, and only one of you will be here next semester,' thing?"

"Did giants walk the earth?"

Laughter. The students clearly like Frank. He likes them. It's a treat to teach them. The bar is filling up and getting loud. Music has changed. Frank says to no one in particular, "This music proves evolution is wrong." Then he remembers his dad saying the same thing about the Beatles. "Fuck, I'm getting old."

The topic shifts to student debt. $60,000 says one, $80,000 another, $100,000 the third. All agree debt plays a big role in their career choices; they can't take a low-paying public interest job. Forget Legal Aid.

"Kay will pay off her loans in the first week."

Kay is the editor of the Law Review. She has a job with a national firm in Phoenix, a starting salary, well over six figures.

"But I'll have to live in Phoenix and do corporate law."

"Poor girl," someone laughs.

"Seriously, I always planned on returning to Flagstaff and working with troubled kids."

"So why take the job?"

"Everyone tells me it's a great job."

Laughter, another round. Meanwhile Sheriff Gary Cooper, having proven he isn't a coward, a craven coward, outdraws the man who hates him and rides off with his bride, Grace Kelly.

Frank rides off in an Uber.

Marie has picked up the kids from school, puts her famous homemade mac and cheese in the oven, Frank makes the salad and sets the table. The traditional hectic family dinner, with Junior's stock answer to all questions, "Not much," and Lilly telling a long story beginning, "And then Billy said" and ending with "Lupe spilled her ice cream." Neither Marie nor Frank have a clue who Billy or Lupe are but feel sad for Lupe.

After they finally get the kids to bed they have some time to relax and catch up. A glass of wine, white for her, red for Frank's heart.

"I'm worried about our son. He might not make the all-star team. It will break his heart," Marie says.

"So, he'll get a PhD in physics."

"I'm serious."

"Your worries never end. If Junior makes the all-stars, you'll worry he isn't starting. Starting, you'll worry he isn't batting three hundred. Batting well, you'll worry he isn't getting along with his friends. I never made all-stars; I was the last chosen and things worked out."

"Have you given any more thought about moving? And don't say you're too busy," Marie says.

"I know a pool would be nice and a bigger house. Maybe we can find something around here. I would hate to leave the neighborhood."

"It's not just about us. It's about our children. Pueblo High is 90 percent Hispanic and I love them all. But you know the biggest influence on kids isn't us, it's peer pressure. Few of the kids here plan on college and you told me a lot of kids around here think it's a right of passage to go to prison, like their uncle did."

"Maybe that's why we should stay. Remember that presentation I gave at the middle school where most of the boys said they wanted to join the military or be cops? And the girls wanted to be hairdressers. Convince the kids they can do more, they can finish high school, go to college. Our children will be a great influence on them."

"I understand what you're saying. It's so confusing. I would hate to bail out. But our kids need a good education."

"Yeah, but I'm not sure being the only Mexican in the school is a great idea, particularly with all the hostility directed at immigrants. I'm sure some smart ass will ask Junior if he's legal."

"That happened last week at Little League. We can't protect them. They're tough. Junior answered, 'I'm legal, are you?' And having smart Mexicans in their class will teach the bigots a thing or two."

"Marie, you said yourself how kids in those fancy schools are killing themselves trying to get into Stanford. All study, no fun. When they were toddlers their parents read them *War and Peace*, not *Dr. Seuss*."

"Frank, you're so clever. That's why I love you."

Frank smiles, finishes his wine. "Integration, diversity, are great ideas in the abstract but a little harder when it comes to your own children, your own neighborhood. I'll have another glass."

"Me too."

CHAPTER THIRTY-NINE

Lucy follows Cindy to her car, a red Lincoln MKX. Unlike her Honda, it is spotless. How can she afford a car like that?

They could walk; it's close, but Cindy suggests they drive. She needs to get back in an hour. "It's not like I have to clock in, but I have lots of work to finish this afternoon. Frank types a lot of his stuff, but Sean uses an old dictating machine. He can be a prima donna."

Salad, Inc. is in, at least this month. You can choose every ingredient you want or don't want. Check a box to order the type of lettuce, choice of veggies, meat, and dressing. Lucy laughs when she gets to dressing— on the side or mixed in, light, average, or extra. Too many choices. Growing up, her mom put the food on the table and you ate it or went hungry. She would've found this place hilarious.

It's been years since her mom died. Lucy still has the urge to phone her when something good happens; when she was accepted at law school, graduated, rescued Teddy, got the job at Perez and O'Grady. Her mom would be happy she's with Clay, someone who's smart and kind. She'd be sorry to miss out on grandkids.

Grandkids? That's a big if. I don't know if I want kids or if Clay does or if the two of us will last. I'm glad mom never knew about my addiction. Maybe she'd be proud I was in recovery. I'll never know.

They turn in their salad orders, pick up their drinks, both black passion fruit iced tea, no sugar, and find a table.

"I was surprised you suggested lunch," Lucy says.

"Why? We work together. Don't tell me you think a lawyer shouldn't waste time eating lunch with someone who's only a secretary?"

"No, it's nothing like that. The opposite. You're gorgeous. Almost intimidating?"

"Don't knock yourself. You're attractive."

Lucy smiles. "Not compared to you."

"I'd rather be smart. In ten years or so I'll just be another has-been. You have a law degree. People look up to you."

"My sister, Ethel, was the pretty one. Blonde, wavy hair, green eyes, perfect features. She's two years younger. A parade of guys came through our house from the time she was twelve. Our relatives called her the pretty sister, and me, the smart sister. When you're a teenager you don't want to be the smart sister."

The waiter arrives with their salads. "Which one of you had the romaine?"

"I did," Lucy answers.

"And you must have the spring mix." He smiles at Cindy, places it carefully in front of her. "Is there anything else I can bring you?" He looks only at Cindy.

"No, it's all fine," Cindy says.

"All you have to do is wave at me if you need anything." He stands there, stares at Cindy as if waiting for her to say something, something like, "Wow, you're cute." She doesn't. He leaves.

Finally.

"See what I have to put up with? Like I care about a kid who works at a glorified salad bar. He isn't even cute."

Lucy tries her salad. Not bad. She's starving, wishes she were eating a burger instead of rabbit food. Someday she'll enjoy it?

"How's it going with you and Clay? You haven't said much about him lately."

"We broke up for a while. I did something stupid. We're back together, but taking it a little slower."

Tell Cindy what I did? She doesn't seem judgmental, but I don't want her to think I'm a snoop and insecure. Maybe when I know her better.

"Do you care about him?"

"I do. He's a terrific person—honest and kind."

"Good for you. Those qualities are hard to find." Cindy eats her salad, she relishes each bite. "What do you think about the law firm?"

"Love it. They're letting me do elder law. Some of the clients are terrific. I wasn't a fan of Harold."

"Looked me over. Flashed his ring. He'll get his. I'm a big believer in karma."

Karma my ass. I don't want to wait that long.

"I hope so."

"Have you been to the veteran's court?" asks Cindy.

"No. Why do you ask?"

"Sean told me about it. It made a big impression on him. I've been thinking about my ex-boyfriend. His birthday was a few days ago. It's ridiculous that I still remember. We broke up years ago."

"Was he in the military?"

"Yeah," says Cindy.

"Tell me about him," says Lucy.

Cindy sips her iced tea. "We started going out sophomore year of high school and soon we were an item. Matt was my first love. He was an awesome boyfriend. Even in high school he'd rather be with me than the guys. We were going to get married after graduation."

"What happened?"

"He joined up. His brother was a Marine, his dad. He never told me that was his plan, but seemed to think I should've known.

"I was OK about it, but I told him I wouldn't marry him till he was discharged. Then he got deployed to Afghanistan. He begged me to marry him before he left. He moved into my place, but that wasn't enough. We had horrible arguments. The weeks before he left were crazy. We had sex a lot. Didn't leave my apartment except to get food. They didn't have deliveries then. When we weren't doing it, he'd try to convince me to marry him."

I should say something but what? Must have been hard when he was in Afghanistan. Duh.

"Matt was different when he got back. I don't know what

happened over there. He wouldn't talk about it. Some of his squad got killed. Most of what I found out was from one of the military wives I'd gotten friendly with."

"How did he change?"

"When he got back he hardly talked to me. He was always angry, at me, at the war, at everyone who wasn't in the war. He couldn't sleep, and when he did he had nightmares. Screamed. He'd wake up sweaty and crying, 'I'm sorry.' I think he was talking to people he killed."

"People he killed?" asks Lucy.

"Yeah, they never tell you *we expect you to kill people* when you sign up. They tell you about skills you can learn and the benefits. People join to learn trades or do service. Matt would go off by himself for days at a time. We were living together, but I hardly saw him. I didn't know where he went. Drank too much, used drugs."

Been there. Done that.

"What finally happened?"

"Matt started acting crazy. I was afraid he was going to hurt me. One minute I'd want him to move out, the next I'd feel guilty. I didn't think it was all his fault. But he refused to get help."

"Did you kick him out?"

"Yeah. One of our high school friends who'd joined the Army but never deployed committed suicide. That put Matt over the edge. Besides yelling, he punched holes in the wall and destroyed stuff. I told him to leave. Matt looked at me like he was going to come after me, but he didn't. He left."

"A guy who didn't deploy killed himself?"

"Turns out guys in the military who don't deploy have a high suicide rate. Survivors guilt plus pressure of being away from home, wondering if they're good enough."

"Sounds horrible."

"It was. In spite of everything I was still in love with him. I didn't go out with anyone for two years. I think he's the reason I never married."

More silence. Both ate.

"Thanks for listening. I guess I needed to talk about him. I never found out what happened to him."

"You could look him up on Facebook."

"No, I don't think so. I need to get on with my life without him." Cindy looks up from her salad, "Dusty is so sweet. I sometimes think about getting a dog, but I never have."

"I have a rescue dog, Teddy. He's still traumatized."

"Where'd you get him?"

"A public defender client got arrested and animal control took his dog. It was very young, still a puppy. The office paid to spring the dog, but when the client was released he split without him. I took him. He was supposed to be a golden retriever, but never grew that big. I think he's a corgi-beagle mix. Cute as can be, but skittish."

"You should bring him to work."

"I don't know if he and Dusty would get along. He can be aggressive with other dogs."

I might get fired if Teddy snarled at a client or, oh my god, bit one. Whatever happened I'd never put him down. Even if it costs my job.

"Bring him, see what happens. He can sit with me when you have a client or conference. We can see how he and Dusty do together. Dusty's good with other dogs."

"I know it's probably none of my business, but you have beautiful clothes and a great car? How can you do that on your salary?"

"My credit cards are maxed. My sister owns Carla's Closet, that second-hand clothing store on Campbell. I get first pick. As for the car, my brother works at the Ford dealership and this car was a trade-in."

"I don't know how we could function without you. You're so smart, do you ever think about doing something different?"

"I'm not that smart."

"You are."

"I never went past high school. People in my family don't go to college."

"Neither did mine. I know lots of people with not much

education who are very smart. Be the first. Start at community college, take a night class or two and see what interests you."

Bobby-Jo would be proud of me.

"I thought about being a special ed teacher until I realized you had to go to four years of college."

"You can do it. You're young. Why teaching?"

"My other brother, not the one who works for Ford, has mental problems. He had a wonderful first-grade teacher who helped him a lot. I'd love to do that for other kids. Sean thought about working in special ed. That's what his mom does. Sean tells me how much she loves her kids."

Sean teaching? He's not that type. But a good sense of humor is important in a teacher. The kids would like him, but still.

"I can't see Sean doing that."

"I can. There's another side of Sean he doesn't show often. He isn't just a womanizer. He can be compassionate and soul-searching. He talks about doing something more with his life than making money. Maybe teaching, even the Peace Corps. He always admired his mother."

Maybe I misjudged him?

"Good to know. You never can tell about people. We better get back or you'll be late."

They leave. The waiter smiles. Cindy doesn't make eye contact.

The waiter loses hope.

Finally.

CHAPTER FORTY

Today is Karen's first drug court hearing. If the heroin had weighed only one-tenth of a gram more she'd be facing mandatory prison. At a seminar she attended, Lucy learned a gram was about the size of a sugar packet. One-tenth of a gram is a very small amount, but it's enough to change a person's life.

Lucy meets Karen at the courthouse. Earlier that morning Karen had met with Sharon, her probation officer.

"I'd expected her to be mean, maybe scary, but she wasn't. She was cool. Acted like she wanted me to succeed."

"All rise, the honorable Lourdes Velasquez presiding,"

The judge, who looks young, sits behind the bench in her black robe, a court clerk next to her. Two lawyers from the public defender's office, who Lucy remembers, Gina and Ruth, sit at the defense table. Few defendants can afford private lawyers. After today Lucy will withdraw from Karen's case and either Gina or Ruth will be assigned to represent her.

Today the defendants are women. Women and men alternate Mondays to avoid the constant flirting and to make women feel comfortable talking about their traumas. Most have experienced sexual abuse, not something they want to talk about in front of men.

"Lynne and Yvonne, come up," Judge Velasquez says. The two women approach the bench. "You're both eligible to graduate." The audience applauds. Most have been in counseling with Lynne and Yvonne and are thrilled when someone they struggled with graduates, except for the envious few.

"For those who don't know, Yvonne only has to finish this

semester to get her AA degree and is working as an assistant at a veterinarian's office. She's been clean 234 days. Lynne works at Ace Hardware, and has gotten her daughter back from foster care. She's been clean 189 days." More clapping. A date for the graduation ceremony is set.

They're not home free yet. Joyce graduated. Harold's still out there.

Next Velasquez calls up several women who are doing well. All are clean, attending counseling, and not in other trouble. Some earned a thirty-, sixty- or ninety-day chip, which commemorates their days of sobriety.

"Brandy Doherty." Her lawyer, Gina, approaches the bench with her. Not a good sign. "You've done well until the last couple weeks. You missed two drops and two counseling sessions." Brandy is skinny, bad complexion, dry hair. Her jeans are very tight and her shirt too big. Her clothes look old and don't quite fit.

"I'm sorry, Judge," tears roll down her face. "My parents kicked me out. I've been staying with friends. I don't have a car."

"Why did your parents kick you out?"

"They think I stole some money from my sister. Every time something goes missing they blame me."

Judge Velasquez says nothing. Tension builds.

"I took the money," Brandy blurts out.

"How much?"

"Only about twenty dollars."

"Are you employed?"

"No, but I think I can find a job this week. My PO has given me names of places that hire people in legal trouble. I've been leaving resumes at those places and anywhere else that's hiring. No one's phoned me back."

"Do you have a place to stay, not a couch at someone's house?"

Brandy and her lawyer confer. Her lawyer isn't pleased.

"She doesn't have a place for sure, but she thinks her grandmother will let her stay. She's retired, a widow, and has an extra bedroom."

"Are you clean?"

Again Brandy and Gina confer.

"No."

"I'm going to sentence you to forty-eight hours jail. If your grandmother agrees you can stay, your probation officer will check out her home, and if probation thinks it's appropriate, you can be released earlier. Brandy, I am also ordering you to pay back your sister. It'd be a good idea to apologize to your family."

"Your Honor, what if I call her grandmother now and she says yes?" Gina asks.

"Probation needs time to assess the situation. If that doesn't work out are you willing to live in a halfway house?"

"OK," says Brandy. It's clear she doesn't want to.

"If your grandmother doesn't work out, I'm ordering probation to try to find you a place in a halfway house. Good luck, Brandy." One of the deputies walks over to Brandy and places her in handcuffs. She's sobbing. The room is still as Brandy is walked out the back door. To the jail cells. Realization kicks in. The women realize if they screw up that would be them.

Could have been me. I used illegal drugs. In rehab I lied, missed counseling, tested positive. I could have been arrested, sent to jail, had a record. I'd never have been a lawyer.

Judge Velasquez continues calling up the women. The rest have messed up one way or another. Rather than jail, most are given additional urine drops, extra counseling, or told to write an essay about what triggers their drug use or what to do if they feel like using.

When the judge completes the other hearings, Karen and two newcomers are called to the bench. "Ms. Portillo, Ms. Sanchez, and Ms. Vance, welcome to drug court. You probably have a good idea about how we operate from your lawyer, PO, and by being here today.

"Let's start by talking about drops. Each of you has been assigned a color. If your color is called you drop. No excuses. You need to call the lab every day to check for your color.

"You'll be required to go to group counseling. Your PO will tell you which group to attend. You'll be in a group with the women you see here. They all want to help you stay clean and you'll want to help them."

Lucy wonders if Karen will make it. Karen and Ms. Sanchez don't look like druggies. Ms. Vance is a mess, skeletal, jittery, like all she's thinking about is where she can get her next fix. Lucy knows that look.

"We're on your side and want you to succeed. If you mess up, which happens, the best thing you can do is ask for help. Don't skip drops. Better to be dirty than miss. Don't skip counseling. Most important, don't ever miss court. You are expected to show up at all your hearings. For now, that will be every other Monday. If you have questions ask your PO or your lawyer. I wish all three of you the best of luck. Court is adjourned."

Working at drug court would be cool. Helping people, not punishing them. I needed help, not punishment.

CHAPTER FORTY-ONE

Lucy looks at the clock. It's time to go. She turns off her computer, grabs her briefcase, and walks several blocks to her Honda. *Shit, a seventy-five-dollar ticket. That's ridiculous. I'm supposed to run to my car every two hours to feed it quarters? Who carries quarters? Why can't they have eight-hour meters, or at least four? Shit.*

She's on her way to meet Jamie, a woman she'd met in rehab. A sad but common story. Happily married, raising two daughters, and then, age forty-five, the roof falls in. Her daughters are off at college and her husband runs off with her best friend. Lost and lonely she turns to alcohol. She hates beer, even wine, only likes sweet drinks like Pina Coladas. But she can't drink more than two. Sugar highs don't make friends or bring happiness.

She starts online dating, meets the wrong people, and is soon popping pills. Weekly, then daily. She knows drugs are bad, she never even tried pot in high school, but drugs do bring momentary happiness and make friends irrelevant. She loses her cashier's job at Safeway. Stops texting her daughters. Concerned, they come home and stage an intervention. She ends up at Serenity House and meets Lucy.

The two talk every couple of weeks and have an occasional dinner. Jamie called yesterday. She didn't sound good. Asked Lucy to meet her at Coffee Exchange, a 24/7 cafe with Wi-Fi close to Jamie's house.

Jamie sits at a table in the back drinking a small coffee. Lucy almost doesn't recognize her. She has lost weight, has black circles around her bloodshot eyes, and looks more like a homeless person than a middle-class mother of two college girls. She gives Lucy a hug. Holds tight.

Lucy goes to the counter and comes back with a latte and a scone for each of them. She waits for Jamie to say something, but she doesn't.

"Are you using?" Lucy asks.

"No, worse. Dealing."

"Dealing? Drugs? How could you?"

"Money. I can only get part-time jobs and the pay sucks. My girls are in college and it's expensive. I told myself if I don't sell it someone else will. People are free to make their own decisions. What crap. I want out. My daughters and I will get by somehow."

"I'm glad to hear you want out. Can I help?"

Jamie trembles. "I'm afraid I'll go to prison. I probably deserve to. And if I quit I'm afraid of what my dealer will do to me. He's part of a cartel."

Lucy holds up her hand to stop Jamie. She knows DAs make deals if defendants name higher ups. Snitching others was controversial at the PDs office. Many lawyers hated it.

"I'm pretty sure if you name names, if you tell who you get the drugs from, you'll avoid prison."

"But I might be hurt or killed?"

"Hopefully they'll arrest the guy and he'll go to prison. The police will protect you, maybe even put you in witness protection if they think it's necessary."

Jamie doesn't say anything for several minutes. Lucy waits.

"Fuck it. I'll take the chance. Some people died. I'd love to rat out Harold."

"Harold? Harold who?"

"Olsen, big real estate honcho."

Lucy smiles. "I think I can help you. But I have to make some calls. Eat your scone." Jamie takes a small bite. "I'll be in touch with you as soon as I get something arranged. Hang in there." They hug again.

The next morning Lucy parks in a pay lot near the office. She's not a slow learner. In the office she checks email, texts, and phone messages. She's working on a sentencing memo about one of Sean's clients who they've named Lester the Molester. Lester will be off to prison; the only question is for how long. Like 80 percent of those in prison, he didn't finish high school.

First things first. She closes her office door and takes out her cell. She doesn't want the firm's number to show. She dials.

"Detective Duffy, narcotics."

"It's Lucy Wagner, you probably don't remember me."

"Sure I do, you're the good-looking one at the Perez firm, the one that sprung that sleaze, Harold Olsen. What can I do ya for?"

Good-looking one. I hope he's not one of those.

"I would like to meet with you. Not your office or mine. For coffee. I have something on Harold Olsen that you might be interested in."

"Like what?"

"One of his dealers might cooperate."

"In an hour. The Cup."

"Make it two. And not downtown, I don't want to run into any colleagues. Starbucks at Glenn and Campbell?"

"Fine. Sounds exciting. Mysterious. I'll wear a red carnation."

Lucy and Jamie are in line when Duffy arrives. Midthirties, good shape, wearing jeans, a faded polo shirt, and a NY Mets baseball cap. No carnation.

"Lucy," whispers Duffy with a stage glance around the room. "It's me. Couldn't find the carnation."

Maybe he's OK.

They take a corner table, far from those absorbed on their computers. Still they talk softly.

"This has nothing to do with my firm or with me being a lawyer. I'm here as a private citizen. This is Jamie. First off we need your to promise you won't arrest her for selling drugs."

"Hold on. What do I get?"

"Maybe Harold Olsen. Jamie's one of his dealers. Promise if she helps you get him you won't go after her."

"I'll be too busy celebrating. Promise."

Does his promise mean anything? Only the DA can make deals. I should have talked to Frank. Am I throwing Jamie to the wolves? No way to know. We've crossed that bridge.

They fall silent. Each waits for the other to make the next move. "Trevor," the barista calls. Duffy winks and goes to pick up their drinks. He always uses a fake name at Starbucks, partly because of his undercover work and partly because he likes thinking he could always be someone else. Trevor would be dashing.

"Olsen sells heroin cut with fentanyl," says Duffy. "People have died. A hot-shot prosecutor wants to indict him for manslaughter, maybe even second-degree murder. You got a deal; Jamie, if you help us, nothing will happen to you."

"Will Harold know I ratted him out?"

"Not before his trial and maybe not then."

Realizing this isn't good enough, Duffy adds, "They probably won't need you as a witness and anyway Harold won't be out for years."

Jamie relaxes, picks up her apricot scone. "Lucy, would you mind buying me a sandwich? I haven't felt much like eating before today."

A sandwich is a small price to pay for getting Harold. Hell, I'd buy her a lobster dinner.

The meeting lasts an hour. "Albert" gets a round of the week's special berry lattes. Albert would be a college prof. Popular with students. Distinguished. Well-known in his field. They turn to planning how to get that fucker. Jamie's information would justify a search warrant, but it'd be better to get him on tape. Jamie agrees to wear a wire, meet him, take the week's delivery, and pay him in marked twenties.

They work fast. Two days later all three are in Duffy's office. He plays the tape.

A man's voice: *Hey babe, how's business?*

Jamie's voice: *Not bad, Harold.*

A man's voice: *You don't look so hot. You're not skimming the product? Can't have my dealers doing that.*

Jamie's voice: *No way. Bad cold. I've got a couple of new customers. I need a couple extra bags.*

A man's voice: *Heroin right? You're in luck. Just got in a shipment. Terrific stuff, cut with a little fentanyl—junkies love it. Better high. Got to watch it, too much fentanyl can be bad, but junkies know drugs are dangerous and it's a free country.*

Jamie's voice: *If they don't get it from us they'll get it from someone else.*

A man's voice, laughing: *Unless we kill that someone else. Be right back with your order. You got the money?*

Jamie's voice: *Of course.*

Duffy turns off the recorder high fives Jamie. "Jesus, you're a pro. You used his name and he admitted knowing about dangers of fentanyl. Manslaughter here we come, or maybe even better."

Jamie smiles. Life is looking up. Maybe she'll get her Safeway job back. But it gets better.

Duffy picks up his phone and puts it on speaker.

"Now watch this. Ralph, Duffy here. You still following Harold?"

"Yes, boss. In the dining room at the Hilton. Looks like a business meeting."

"There is a god. Arrest him now. Recite the charges, selling drugs and manslaughter. Loudly. In front of his friends. Cuff him. Real tight."

Lucy smiles.

And Sean calls me "Mary Poppins."

CHAPTER FORTY-TWO

Lucy walks into Ike's, a downtown coffee shop and cafe that features numerous kinds of espresso coffee drinks, pastry, soups, salads, and sandwiches. Lawyers swarm, getting their last latte before returning to court. It's only two blocks. Ike's only has a few tables, does a heavy volume in takeout. Monday is "law and motion day," no trials but courtrooms filled with lawyers arguing summary judgments, statutes of limitations, and accusing each other of discovery abuse. Lucy had planned to get a sandwich and eat it back at the office. Lately she's worked through lunch. Worth it if she gets a permanent job.

"Hi, Lucy," says Ruth, one of the drug court lawyers. Gina is the other. She knows them, but not well, from the PD, and she'd observed them when she took Karen to drug court.

"Join us if you're not busy."

"Love too. I'll order and be right back."

Gina in her thirties, Ruth in her forties, neither wears trial garb. No suits or dresses with jackets. Instead casual slacks and shirts. PDs argue about appropriate work dress. Some believe it's important to look professional. You get respect. Gina and Ruth have joined the con faction who believe it's more important to bond with their clients. Gina and Ruth's parents were war protestors in the sixties. Both told their children about demonstrations, free speech ad infinitum. They skipped the free love and LSD parts. Neither thought any of it rubbed off, but some must've.

Gina has a large green salad and Ruth's looks like a fancy BLT.

"How's your new job going?"

"Pretty good. I like the people I work with and there's a firm dog."

"Firm dog—how cool is that? What kind?"

"Dusty's a golden retriever. Real sweetheart."

"I'd love to bring my dog to work. She's a rescue half lab, half pit, but she's not very well behaved," says Gina.

"Like any dog you've ever owned is well behaved," says Ruth. "If I recall you got kicked out of dog training classes because you refused to discipline one of your dogs."

"Lucy, don't you miss the fun lunches and the crude jokes?" Gina says in an attempt to change the subject.

"Had lunch with the group a couple of weeks ago. Love the people, but don't you get angry about the jokes?"

Ruth takes a bite of her sandwich. "I complained once and never heard the end of it. Management made everyone watch a film on sexual harassment which was, unfortunately, a little like *Reefer Madness*. After the film that sleaze Art said, 'I learned some new tricks.' You doing mostly criminal?"

"It's not just the guys," Gina interrupts. "Deanne has a bigger potty mouth than anyone. One of the newbies came out of a staff meeting and said, 'I was raised in a religious family. I never heard a woman talk like that.' He was going to complain about her, but the guys harassed him so much he withdrew it. Now he swears like a sailor."

"I'm doing a lot of elder law. It's more my thing than criminal."

"Wills," says Ruth. "When I was law student I volunteered at a neighborhood law office and a woman wanted a will. I told her I wasn't a lawyer but she insisted. So I wrote one for her. I've been haunted for the last twenty years thinking I screwed up and the will's no good."

"Not to mention practicing law without a license," says Gina.

"I was impressed when I brought my client to drug court," says Lucy. "You guys all work like a team. And the judge seemed concerned about the clients."

"She's great. Judges don't get assigned to drug court. They volunteer. A lot of judges think it's too much like social work and they're too smart for that kind of assignment. I heard Judge Velasquez had a close family member OD on heroin. Maybe that's why she volunteered. Who was your client?"

"Karen Portillo."

"Yeah, she's mine," says Gina. "Nice girl. I think she'll make it."

"You guys remember a client named Jamie?" asks Lucy. "She's a friend of mine."

"Who?" asks Gina.

"Jamie Higgins."

"Yeah, she graduated. How's she doing?"

"Rough period, but doing better."

Shit I can't tell them she was dealing and about Harold. No way.

"Not unusual. We do our best to help people get their lives back. Because we're lawyers they usually listen to us. The fear of god and jail. But sometimes it doesn't work."

"There's a downside," says Ruth. "You get close to some of the defendants and end up going to a lot of funerals."

Joyce. Should I tell them I was, am, an addict? Maybe if things don't work out at the firm I can try to get a job in drug court. Being a recovering addict might be a plus.

"Would you mind explaining the ins and outs of how drug court works? Other than taking my client to a hearing I'm in the dark."

"Be glad to," says Gina. "But if you want you can come to staffing and watch, we could arrange it. I'm sure the judge will be OK with it. As long as you understand everything in staffing is confidential."

"That would be cool. What's a staffing?"

"We have a staffing before each drug court. The drug court POs, Ruth and I, the drug court coordinator, and sometimes a counselor or two will come. We discuss each person who is scheduled to appear. Are they clean? Did they go to counseling? Did they get in any other trouble? Are they working? And did they pay their fees?

"The POs make recommendations for sanctions, an essay on what triggers using, extra urine drops, additional counseling, or jail. Jail is saved for serious violations like missing drops or counseling twice. It's normally a max of forty-eight hours. If we disagree with the recommendation we try to get the judge to change it. Often she does."

Gina adds, "Some of the POs are terrific. They care about the clients; but some are too punitive. They don't get that a relapse is part of recovery or how hard it is to quit. And most of the defendants have no money, no job; they commute by bus because they don't have a car or even a license and have a hard time making appointments."

"You're lucky," Lucy says. "It's lots of work, but you help people. If I don't get a permanent job, maybe I could do that. If you had a spot."

"There are some downsides to working in drug court. You'll never get a raise and likely be one of the lowest paid in the office. We're not held in very high regard because we're not 'trial lawyers.'"

"I hear appellate lawyers are also underpaid."

"They still make more than us."

"I don't need much. My dog isn't a picky eater."

They laugh.

"There might be openings in the future. There is a lot of movement in creating specialty courts aimed at helping rather than punishing."

"I know. One of the guys in our office, Sean, volunteers at vet court and can't stop talking about it."

"Sean's a good friend of mine. He thinks the world of you, told me you were doing a great job."

Sean? I wouldn't be surprised if Frank said that, but Sean? Maybe things will work out.

CHAPTER FORTY-THREE

After four or five months, the heat breaks. Finally. People leave their air-conditioned caves, tables appear on restaurant patios, and tennis starts at eight in the morning instead of six.

Sean walks back to the office. He just lost a drunk driving case. The jury was out thirty minutes. There must have been a fight about who would be foreperson. While Sean goes back to his office his client Dennis goes to jail. He'll be handcuffed, photographed, and given a raggedy orange jumpsuit that's either too big or too small, old, stained, and torn — hopefully not in an embarrassing spot.

It's Dennis' second DUI, so three months in jail, no license for ninety days, and for a year, a device in his car that won't let it start if it smells booze. One more for the road: $10,000 in fines, $15,000 for your lawyer.

Sean isn't too upset. It hurts if you lose when the client is innocent—not so much when they're guilty. Sean is sympathetic when his client gets a first DUI. Can happen to anyone. Even him. But a second? Should've learned your lesson the first time. Called an Uber. Get drunk at home. He'd done a terrific job. He got the arresting officer to admit that evaluating the field sobriety tests is subjective (Dennis fell down only once), that the field tests cannot be replicated (thankfully), and that people taking certain medications would do badly (Dennis wasn't). He also was pleased with his cross of the state's expert, "Yes, the intoxilyzer is not 100-percent accurate" (given Dennis's reading it would have to be only 50-percent accurate).

Despite these setbacks Sean felt he was still in the "reasonable doubt" game as long as the jury didn't understand the jury instructions.

Then they played the video.

When he gets back to the office Cindy greets him. "How long was the jury out?"

"Don't ask."

Cindy smiles, "It's safe to drive again. Mothers Against Drunk Driving should give you a medal. Dennis always stunk of booze. The gang's in the library."

Frank, Lucy, and Dusty, tail wagging, circling under the table. Treats? Big brown eyes reminding his people of their part of the bargain.

"Sean, you're back fast not guilty?" asks Frank.

"Screw you, the best Dennis could hope for was justice delayed."

"You should have taken Trial Practice 101. Lucy, I hear you brought in three cases."

Three new cases. Permanent job?

"Basic estate planning. Interesting people—United Airlines pilot, a brain surgeon, and a high school soccer coach."

"No women?" smiles Sean.

"Only one man, the soccer coach," smiles Lucy.

"I brought in two new divorces," says Frank. "And a bankruptcy."

"Bankruptcy?" Sean feigns shock. "You don't know anything about bankruptcy."

"It's not General Motors. Just some poor guy, totally judgment proof: two Visas, a Master Card, and an American Express. Should've known better. They won't even bother to contest it."

"Fee up front?" asks Sean.

Frank smiles and nods. "Speaking of bankruptcy, we're keeping our heads above water, but maybe not for long. Need new computers—I wish those geniuses at Apple would stop improving things, every time our landlord drives by and sees a client's car, he talks raising the rent, and we promised Cindy a raise."

Need new computers. Higher rent. Shit. There goes my job. Last in, first out. Cindy does deserve a raise.

"Sean, one of my friends at the DA's office told me one of your old clients isn't doing so well," Frank says. "Harold Olsen's in jail. His cartel buddies didn't put up the million-dollar bail. I guess they don't trust him either."

"No bail between thieves." Sean smiles.

"He's facing twenty-five years for selling drugs and manslaughter."

Lucy doesn't smile. Doesn't say a word.

They don't know what I did. Never will. At least I did some good while here. But helping send an ex-client to prison might raise eyebrows. Sean calls me, "Mary Poppins." If he only knew.

"He won't do well in prison," Frank says. "No women, no fancy cars, no more Mr. Olsen. Now he's number 107656. He'll be lucky to get clean sheets."

"A good-looking guy like Harold, soon they'll be bloody sheets," Sean chuckles.

Lucy shakes her head, but is tempted to smile. "Gross."

Dusty's hunger not assuaged, he walks back to his bed. Being a dog isn't a piece of cake.

"Any other business?" Frank asks. "If not, I want to read something to you."

Frank searches his desk for a folder. Sean calls Dusty, but is ignored.

"Have I told you guys I'm teaching writing in prison?"

"Only about five hundred times," sighs Sean.

"Some of the stuff they write is truly remarkable. One paragraph and we can get back to work." He begins to read.

"One day my cellmate asked what I did. Told him I shot a guy. Admitted it, but I really didn't. I told him I was high on drugs. He looked at me, 'You were high on drugs, but you did it.' I was drunk. 'You were drunk, but you did it.' I didn't mean to. 'You didn't mean to, but you did it.' My homies called me a pussy. 'They called you a pussy, but you did it.'"

Frank looks up, pauses. "He ends it with, *'I did it.'* "

Harold, I did it!

CHAPTER FORTY-FOUR

Frank peeks into Sean's office.

"What's up, partner?"

"Reading the city's zoning code and the state statute dealing with liquor licenses. One of my clients is thinking of opening a laundromat that sells beer, 'Suds and Buds.' "

"Great idea. If he has big screen TVs playing sports he'll be a godsend to women, men will do laundry. Speaking of beer, let's get a quick one. Been a while. I have a couple of things we need to talk about."

Shit, why not just a beer? 'Need to talk.' Sounds ominous. Dissolving the partnership? Illness? Divorce?

"Be with you in a second. The Drunken Chicken?"

"Yeah. We took the kids there last week. Never thought I'd like fried chicken and waffles. The kids loved the dessert waffle, filled with chocolate chips and topped with ice cream and tons of whipped cream."

The Chicken is one of Sean's favorites, numerous draft beers in the heart of his favorite part of town, the hippie part. Long hair, weird garb, panhandlers, two blocks of used clothing stores, a variety of eateries, smoke shops, tattoo parlors, a bookstore, and a hip novelty shop selling T-shirts with a picture of Jesus saying, 'I didn't say that.'

They take a seat in a booth near the back. A few men at the bar are getting a tad loud. It's five o'clock somewhere an hour ago. TVs on three walls, all on different channels. Talking heads on one, the replay of last night's game on another and, due to bartender neglect, the third pitching "life-changing" pillows.

"Have you decided about moving to the foothills?" Sean asks.

"Tough decision. We go round and round and we're not sure what side we're on anymore. We won't move till school's out so we have time."

The waitress appears. Frank orders a Tecate and Sean an iced tea and gives the waitress his card. "Run a tab."

"That's a first," Frank smiles.

"I might stay. The waitress is a knockout. What do you want to talk about? Are we broke?"

"Doing pretty well. But you still flirt with Cindy too much. You gotta stop. Lucy doesn't like it either. We don't want to get sued."

"Fine. I started seeing someone a couple weeks ago. She's a personal trainer, good-looking, fun."

"God, Sean, can't you find someone who can read?"

"That's pretty stereotypical. Kim has a master's degree in German literature. Teaches junior college classes."

"Maybe culture will rub off."

It would be great if she could explain Nietzsche.

"Last weekend we saw a foreign film, one with subtitles. It had a plot — no car chases or zombies."

"I'm impressed." Frank checks the time. "I want to talk about Lucy. She's been working hard, bringing in business. Maybe we should make her a partner or if not, let her go. She can find another job."

Good news. No illness, no divorce, no bankruptcy. We survived another month. Lucy's a good lawyer. Frank's right.

"She has been talking about the drug court lawyers and how much good they do. Maybe she can get a job with the PD," says Sean.

The waitress appears, short skirt, skimpy top, smiles. "Another?"

Frank says no. The waitress is asking Sean.

"You're a lawyer, aren't you? Haven't I seen you on TV?"

"Not recently. What's your name?"

"Jody, and yours?"

"Sean."

She smiles. "I love the name Sean. I love everything Irish. If you want to talk I'm off at seven." She walks away slowly, hips swaying.

"Jesus, Sean, five minutes ago you told me you started dating this terrific girl, Kim."

"She's at a conference tonight." Sean pauses, smiles, "I'm kidding. I'm not hitting on anyone. I promise. And I'll leave Cindy to her hoards of admirers. As for Lucy, she should be used to crude jokes, she worked at the public defender's."

"I don't think that's a defense to a sexual harassment claim, 'Where she worked was worse.' "

All the seats at the bar are full. Now it's five o'clock in Tucson. Jody is busy but not too busy to hand Sean a folded piece of paper. He opens it. Her phone number.

Frank looks disgusted. "Someday you're going to have to grow up."

"Time to put away childish things?"

"I never knew you went to church. Funny how it never came up."

"I didn't go to church much," Sean says. "Took a great course, the Bible as Literature, insightful stuff, came away with some wonderful quotes to use in college essay tests."

"My parents didn't give us a choice. Wasn't glad then but am now. We take the kids every Sunday. They enjoy it. Dressing up. Kids. Donuts. How are your parents?"

"Doing fine. Fighting Walmart and loving the grandkids. Sometimes I think I should have stayed, worked with my dad in the hardware store, hung out with high school friends."

"One reason I don't want to move is that I don't want to lose contact with my high school friends. You never get friends like that again."

Sean nods.

I wonder how Kinsey and Larry are. I should look them up, become Facebook pals. Maybe I should have stayed and got involved in politics. Maybe I'd be mayor and worry about potholes rather than whether a mother can get her adult disabled child on welfare.

"Why make Lucy a partner?"

"She's smart, works hard, gets along with clients, brings in business and has close ties with the lawyers at the public defender's. And recovering addicts have legal problems. Money's tight, but she'll carry her weight. Not to mention we don't want to be the last all-male firm standing, she's female."

"I never would've noticed. You're Mexican, I'm Irish. Can't get more diverse than that. See any problems with her?"

Frank looks at the TV. The blond, earnest pillow pusher has been replaced by a serious woman suggesting you sue your back surgeon for trying, operators standing by.

"Not sure we want to get into elder law."

"Frank, go to a basketball game. Nothing but grey heads. A growth industry. And they can afford lawyers. I am thinking of moving into that field myself. Good change of pace."

"It's hard, estate planning, guardianships, trusts, will contests, retirement, pay issues, elder abuse. You'll spend your life taking CLEs."

Suing surgeons gives way to organic, gluten-free cat food that will make your cat healthy and happy, "Playful like the kitten you fell in love with."

"I know Lucy's been clean a long time. But she was an addict. If she becomes a big part of our practice and falls off the wagon, we're—to coin a phrase—fucked."

"Come on, Frank. Maybe she'll get pregnant. Maybe she'll run off and join the circus. Maybe I will."

Frank stares at Sean. "People with substance abuse issues can be real problems."

Silence.

"Frank, you're the one who suggested a beer. I haven't had a drink in two weeks," Sean says, expecting high praise, the high praise he surely deserves.

He gets a laugh instead.

"Marie said you needed a good woman. Kim must be something. We'll talk more." Frank gets up to leave and Sean goes to pay the bill.

Maybe Lucy's too much of a risk. I haven't had a beer in two weeks but want one. Those guys at the bar drinking as if their beers are no big deal. I felt like grabbing them and telling them to pay attention, to enjoy. I don't know if I can stay off booze and maybe Lucy won't be able to stay off drugs. Those pillows looked pretty damn good.

CHAPTER FORTY-FIVE

The next few days aren't great for Lucy. Her United Airlines pilot was transferred to Chicago, the soccer coach never showed, and Karen's father, while thankful she's in drug court, is reluctant to pay the bill. "She should have kept her public defender. I'm not made of money." *Maybe the firm can't keep me on. They'll never let Cindy go. And what's with Sean telling me he's given up drinking and asking about relapse? Does he think I'm using? And spending time in Frank's office behind closed doors. They never close the door except for client conferences.*

Her phone buzzes. "Lucy, can you come into the library? Important meeting." Frank sounds serious.

I'm fucked. Don't cry.

Frank sits at one end of the table. Cindy to his right and Sean standing, looking out the window. They stop talking when she walks in. It's quiet.

"Sit down, Lucy." Frank points to the chair at the other end of the table.

Hold it together. Act professional.

"Who brought the donuts?" Lucy asks, wanting to appear cheerful. "Trying to ruin my diet?"

"Lucy, forget the donuts. We have to make serious changes in the office," Frank says. Cindy looks down and Sean continues to look out the window.

Maybe they're not letting me go, maybe they're firing me. Found out about Harold. I might be disbarred. Humiliated. What will people think? My friends will dump me. Drugs are my friends. One wonderful hit never hurt.

Dusty, sensing Lucy's anxiety, walks over and sits close to her. Dusty is a good dog. No one makes eye contact. Lucy's about to cry.

Why don't they say something?

She blurts out, "Tell me already."

Cindy shakes her head. "You bastards, tell her."

Sean turns, smiles, "Congrats! Lucy, you're a partner."

"What? Say that again."

"You're a partner."

Cindy hands her a business card. 'Perez, O'Grady, and Wagner.'

A job. New car. Clothes. Dentist. Clay will be happy for me. Teddy, too.

"Should read, 'O'Grady, Perez, and Wagner' but, oh well," Sean says, "I lost the coin flip. It should've been two out of three."

"Should be 'Wagner, Perez, and O'Grady,' " Cindy laughs.

"I can't believe it. Such a great place to work. I love you guys. And Dusty." She pats Dusty.

Can I bring Teddy to work? He's a good dog. I'll have to get a new dress or two. Maybe trade in the Honda. I only wish my mother were alive. I can't wait to tell Clay. Cindy thinks Dusty will get along with Teddy. Maybe two is too many dogs. Won't get much for the Honda. Teddy barks if he gets anxious. What if he did something bad?

"I thought I was getting fired."

"Close call," Sean smiles. "You're a great lawyer. Whoever called you 'Mary Poppins' was an idiot. You won't get rich or be famous, be lucky if you get on TV, Frank killed the NFL ad." He winks at Cindy. Probably not actionable.

Cindy forces a smile and Lucy laughs, "Men."

Frank opens a bottle of champagne. Cindy runs over and hugs Lucy, "I've known for a few days. Hard not to tell you. I'm so glad you're going to be part of us, *boss*." Both laugh. Hug again.

Frank pours the champagne. "And you, Sean, time to get over your existential angst. It's boring. Remember Lopez? Went to Harvard, a kid from South Tucson. He did great, editor of the Harvard Law Review. We should have had a parade. He could have been a senior partner in a national firm, a high government official, or even a renowned professor. Know what he did?"

Frank pauses, takes a sip of champagne. He learned in high school drama that falling silent brings the audience to the edge of their seats. Who needs Trial Practice 101?

"He came back. Opened a small practice in South Tucson. Did landlord tenant, personal injury, family law, probate, advised friends starting businesses. Went to his retirement dinner last week. He said he is proud of his career, that he helped hundreds—no, thousands—of people through troubled times."

Another sip, another pause. "He said only family doctors can do more."

"Frank, a wonderful story, but no one should get over existential angst. Remember what Socrates said about the unexamined life. We can't win them all, but being with clients in troubled times ain't bad. Until something better comes along being a lawyer ain't bad. For every Harold," he turns to Lucy, "there's a Mary Smith holding her granddaughter."

"There you go again," says Frank. He raises his glass. "To lawyers, in good times great jokes, in bad times great friends. To Lucy, our wonderful new partner, to Cindy who knows more law than any of us, and to us being lawyers." They raise their glasses.

Cindy holding hers high, "And to two of the best bosses, better make that three, and to our hero dog, Dusty."

Dusty, hearing his name, alerts.

Dinner?